Prairie, Dresses, Art, Other

Coffee House Press books are available to the trade through our primary distributor, Consortium Book Sales & Distribution, cbsd.com or (800) 283-3572. For personal orders, catalogs, or other information, write to info@coffeehousepress.org.

Coffee House Press is a nonprofit literary publishing house. Support from private foundations, corporate giving programs, government programs, and generous individuals helps make the publication of our books possible. We gratefully acknowledge their support in detail in the back of this book.

LIBRARY OF CONGRESS CATALOGING-IN-PUBLICATION DATA

Names: Dutton, Danielle, 1975- author.
Title: Prairie, dresses, art, other / Danielle Dutton.
Description: Minneapolis : Coffee House Press, 2024.
Identifiers: LCCN 2023039644 (print) | LCCN 2023039645 (ebook) | ISBN 9781566897037 (paperback) | ISBN 9781566897044 (e-book)
Subjects: LCGFT: Literature.
Classification: LCC PS3604.U775 P73 2024 (print) | LCC PS3604.U775 (ebook) | DDC 800--dc23/eng/20231205
LC record available at https://lccn.loc.gov/2023039644
LC ebook record available at https://lccn.loc.gov/2023039645

PRINTED IN CANADA

31 30 29 28 27 26 25 24   1 2 3 4 5 6 7 8

Prairie, Dresses, Art, Other

Danielle Dutton

COFFEE HOUSE PRESS

Minneapolis

2024

Prairie

Dresses

Art

Other

Prairie

NOCTURNE

From the backseat her son explains what would happen if she got sucked into a black hole. Moon-faced flowers are wild sweet potato with heart-shaped leaves and hairy seeds, white and alive in the night. "It's a perfect example of exponential growth," he says. In summer the light stays long, cicadas apocalyptic with the windows rolled down. Fast down the hill toward the river, heading home. On the opposite bank an oil refinery spreads into Kentucky, its tall stacks shooting flames into the sky. "Imagine your body being split in two halves," he says. West Virginia is wild. It's right there on the signs: *montani semper liberi*. *Montani semper liberi* means mountains are always free? "Then imagine both halves of your body being split in half, and those halves being split in half, then those halves being split in half, and then those halves being split in half. So you'd just keep splitting your pieces until you were only molecules." You were only molecules, she thinks. And those sweet potato flowers like a million wagging moons. "Mom?" he says. "Are you listening?" In a story she read last week at the beach a man in a straw hat cut off a duck's head while the children stood and watched. "Lid—lid—lid—" the man called. "Qua—qua—qua—" said the duck. Then the head fell to the grass and the duck's feet ran its bottom half away. "Yes," she tells him. "Yes!" She shouts over the wind.

It's the hottest week in the world. In Sweden a forest fire has crossed the Arctic Circle. In Oman the overnight low is 120 degrees. Near a small German town famous for its asparagus, long-deserted bombs are exploding beneath the trees. And just downstream in Czechia a hunger stone has emerged in the Elbe, the water having hit a record low. "If you see me, weep," it reads, the words etched desperately four centuries before. A second message emerges upriver: "We cried—We cry—And you will cry." But the dead are loud as toasters. The fish flap in the mud. Meanwhile, farther north, seen only from the sky, ghostly landscapes rise up via drought: the blueprint of an eighteenth-century mansion on a lawn, a World War II airfield beneath a Hampshire farm, an elaborate Victorian garden long ago cut down. Looking at the drone shot of that non-house on her phone, she thought of pressed flowers gone brown—no, those cyanotypes of seaweed she saw once on display. A woman named Anna Atkins had laid carefully dried specimens on chemically treated paper. Left out in the sun, the seaweed burned its own pale shadow onto a deep-blue page. The smell of Kentucky is flammable, damp. The refinery like a spaceship. "This Blue Drama" that exhibition was called.

"In 1672," her son informs her, "a man named Robert Boyle read an entire magazine by the light coming off a piece of rotting veal." From Delaware to Kentucky, they've counted fifteen dead deer by the side of the road. Once the sun set, the deer began to glow. "It was a neck," he says. "It was this disgusting fatty piece of baby cow neck." At a cement table by a grassy field they eat warm melon and pretzels and hard-boiled eggs. A red-winged blackbird trills on a stalk. An old man in the darkened lot moves toward them like a glacier. "I love summer," her son says, oblivious to the stranger, listening to cicadas ringing on and on. "We should just keep driving to wherever it's summer, and when it's not summer there we should drive to wherever it's summer next." The air is thick with meadow grass and bugs. On the one hand, on the highway, traffic rushes past, but pale moths twist over the field as if there were no time. A part of her whorls outward with those moths, out and out to native plants as weedy as her kid—a crooked-stem aster, a blazing star. When she was small, smaller than he is now, and quiet, much quieter than him, her mother wallpapered their apartment in a stylized jungle print. The leaves on the banana trees curled away like ribs. The eyes of the jungle cats looked out like human eyes. Every night when the lights clicked off she saw men stepping between the leaves and right off of the walls.

At last, the stranger has arrived. "Hello," she says. Her son turns. The old man opens a toothless mouth. He is trying to tell them something, and they are trying to hear it, but it takes him thirty years to get it out. "I know," she says when he is done. He turns his gaze to the clamorous field. "No," he shakes his head, "you've got a long way to go."

Night comes to Kentucky with red clouds and green sky and then the fields are flat. No breeze blows. Some satellites shine. With the old man asleep in the seat beside her and her son asleep in the back, she is the only one to see the electric billboard in the middle of nowhere that says JESUS RECYCLED HUMANS. The road rises up. Two weeks at her mother's house has emptied her all the way out. O house in Delaware, bought by a dead husband. O house, a vast expanse of white. That first morning she'd stepped into the yard and everything was wrong—pool, umbrella, plastic shark. As if she'd never been there. "On the rocks?" her mother hissed before even brewing coffee. Several minutes ticked away as she waited for panic to pass. But the sun was clearly rising on the wrong side of that yard. Or else she'd woken back-to-front, and this was what it was like to face the ass-side of your mind. The road rising steeply, the trees nearer the road, the moon like a beacon now between sweet gum and ash and pine. In Pennsylvania there's a house made of glass where you can stand in one spot and watch the sunset and the moonrise at the exact same time. How comforting it sounds. Up on a hill, surrounded by woods, invisible from the road. "Who'd want to live in an invisible house?" rings her mother's voice in her mind. Then a neon something flashes past. And she remembers a half-forgotten class about the beginning of everything back before the bang. A whole semester of lectures on the origin of the world—a yawning gap there was, to start, and regions of fire and frost, and salt, but nowhere grass. In every direction the fields run gray, as if the night absorbed their green, but once upon a time all matter and light were one— then the stars and then the fireflies and then the grass. She has no idea of the time. The clock on the dashboard tells her it's tomorrow. She searches out her phone on the floor, but the car swerves, surprising her, and the old man stirs in his sleep.

For hours the road just goes. Traffic has thinned and her mind makes little visits to that story she read at the beach. "Oh, but I do want to be a bee frightfully," said the girl called Kezia, who sometimes dreamed of camels. But she wasn't allowed to be a bee. She had to pick something else if she wanted to play the game: a rooster, a bull, a donkey, a sheep. Then when she'd raised her eyes from the book it was as if the story had dreamed the bees. Tiny golden bees were hovering above the sand. And the waves were going wild, since somewhere out there a tropical storm was turning and headed in. So they fled her mother's house, days of endless rain—fast through West Virginia and Kentucky heading home.

It's the hottest week in the world. In Siberia the permafrost is collapsing into holes. In California the tide at night blooms an eerie blue. A wildfire in Texas caused a storm with three-inch hail. Then a billboard warns her HELL IS REAL and like a joke the road descends to another giant refinery and its pipe stacks shooting flames into the sky. All is passing memory, she thinks. In the largest of those Siberian holes, what scientists term a "mega slump," they've discovered an ancient forest and plants untouched by the light of the sun for 45,000 years. The locals are afraid. They call the slump a door and claim it makes sounds in the dark. Their hands are cracked and shaking. Who wants to crawl inside? As they cross the melting tundra, the ground beneath their boots turns to jelly with every step. First it's one hole and then another and then at the bottom of the deepest hole they find a frozen lake. The ice is black and solid, but someone sees something inside, deep inside that lake. He gets down on his hands and knees, brushes away the snow. "Look!" she calls, she can't help herself—sparks from that refinery are drifting through the night sky like luminescent plankton. The old man's toothless mouth expels cool air and bats. "Where are we?" cries a voice in the car. The road begins to curve. They are driving upside down on the bottom of the planet. She wishes she could tell him the truth. She says, "We're almost home."

There were five parts to this story, but one of them got lost. It was difficult to keep each strand in her mind, even as it was happening, and then later—no.

To begin with, they were camping. This whole story happens at night, the first night of their first camping trip of the season. It was only mid-March but hot as June, so they booked a site at a campground in the Ozarks. Actually, she booked the site, picking this park because it boasted three promising trails they could choose from in the morning: one that took them past the remains of old mining operations for barite, one with dolomite bluffs, and one that wound through a field of Mississippian petroglyphs. "The location of mysterious prehistoric rituals," she read aloud from the website. But they couldn't leave until after their son's swim practice on Friday, itself after school, so they didn't get to the campsite until basically dinnertime. The sky was a dull gray. Her husband wrestled the tent and she was unpacking the cooler when the custodian of the campground drove up in a golf cart. "Hunting mushrooms?" he asked, nodding toward their son, who was just then disappearing into the woods behind the site. "I think he's gathering kindling," she said, though she didn't know, just wandering off, probably looking for rocks. "Can't do that," said the man. "Not supposed to burn the wood around here. I can sell you some. Six dollars a bag." "Sure," her husband said, stepping in to pay the man, who handed over an orange plastic net heavy with logs. Then he listed the park's amenities and rules— recycling cans, white-nose syndrome. "Stay out of the caves," he said. He wore a bright-red cap with embroidered block letters that spelled MAKE AMERICA GREAT AGAIN. She'd never actually stood in front of someone wearing that hat. "I read about the petroglyphs," she said when he was done. "Do you know anything about the rituals connected to the site?" The man shrugged. "Official word is the rocks give directions for a game, something like Indian baseball." "Indian baseball?" she said. "All the same," he added, "some folks will tell you those marks are a sort of a curse." She smiled out of habit. "Is that a joke?" she asked. But his phone rang and he drove away. The cloud cover had cracked. Fat white clouds were racing east, and the sun was out, though low. The boy was not yet back. The sun was so low, in fact, that the woods— she saw bluebells poking up through a crust of last autumn's leaves—were glowing a greenish-gold. "He's probably looking for rocks," she said, popping a grape into her mouth, but her husband didn't respond, clearing the fire pit of spiders. It had been this warm for weeks, so she was pleased to see the bluebells still more or less on schedule. *Bluebells, cockleshells, eevy, ivy, over. My mother said I never should play with the fairies in the wood.* "It's pretty here," she said, but it was also quiet. No humming RVs. No barking dogs. No kids screaming with glee. Other than her husband, who appeared beside her at the picnic table snapping a can of beer—"Get a load of that asshole's hat?" he said—she couldn't see or hear anyone at all.

After dinner, her husband and son went together to brush their teeth. Though she'd looked at the map online, she hadn't realized she was booking the site closest to the bathrooms. "It'll be nice," she said when they pulled up. "If we need to pee in the middle of the night we can just pop over." But it wasn't nice, and she knew it, and knew what her husband thought. Plus the lights in the bathrooms didn't turn off, so their site wasn't completely dark even after sundown. "Light is pollution," the boy had informed them while eating his campfire nachos. There was a laundry room there too, with someone's shoes tumbling loudly in a dryer—so *somebody* else was there—and the chemical stink of dryer-sheet flowers blowing on the air. Alone, she looked up through the trees. The sky was a blacker black than they ever saw at home. "The night has a thousand eyes," she remembered, "and the day but one." This night had more like a trillion eyes, a zillion. No doubt she should be stirred. No doubt she should be having some sort of epiphanic dawning. Instead, on a log, swatting at something stinging her arm, she took out her phone and pulled up a clip on YouTube about the blackest black paint in the world. "It's like you could literally disappear into it," spoke a disembodied British voice. A man was painting a circle on an empty concrete floor. "So light-absorbing it bends your brain." Then there it was, absorbing all light, a black hole in the palm of her hand. One of her students had died that week. Eighteen years old, over from China, just trying to cross a street. She hadn't been able to sleep, thinking of his parents, still thousands of miles away. Thinking of something he'd written for class about a woman and a piano. Then her brain bent as the woods rang with the sound of a drop of water. "Was that a bird?" she called. Two backlit figures were walking down the path.

The second part is the story their son told by the campfire. He'd been researching cryptids for a school report and had drawn her a picture of his favorite, Mothman, which she'd hung on her office wall. The drawing showed a large rectangle with two sad eyes and no mouth. The rectangle had legs and arms but where its hands should be were wings, and it stood alone on a rock before a vista of conical hills. "It's November in the year 1966," his face a shadowy landscape from the flashlight below his chin. "Two men are digging a grave at a cemetery in West Virginia. It's a moonless night and they're almost done when something big swoops over their heads then flies off into the woods. In the morning they tell everyone in town. The first guy says it looked like a devil with flaming eyeballs, but the other guy just keeps calling it 'the dark creature,' and . . ."

The story continued with a young couple out driving the following night between the same cemetery and an old World War II facility that had manufactured TNT. Then more witnesses and a suspected government cover-up: toxic waste, five-legged deer, the ponds in the woods near the TNT site had turned pink. The mayor told everyone the creature was a migrating crane. The milkman said its eyes flashed like the lights on a bike. An old lady blamed it for the buzzing sounds coming out of her TV. The pastor's dog was mutilated. One family even moved. All this went on for a year. "Someone described it," the boy said, "like watching a horror movie and waiting for the terrible thing to happen, kind of wishing it would happen, like wishing you could get it over with, but then you realize you're inside the movie, so this is your actual life." Finally, on the Friday before Christmas, 1967, during the evening rush hour, the bridge that connected their town to the next began violently to shake, flipped once, and collapsed into the river. Forty-six people died in the icy Ohio. "Of course they blamed it on 'the dark creature,'" he said, "which they claimed they never saw again. And one of the ones who died was a little boy wearing a suit." Then he shook the flashlight all around the campsite. "So how come they call it Mothman," she asked, shielding her eyes, "if everyone thought it looked like a bird?" "How should I know?" he said, and he snapped off the light.

It was only recently he'd turned into this stranger, or some hybrid of a stranger and the boy she used to know. Last weekend, with her husband away again for work, he'd sulked on the couch for an hour before she finally got him to talk. "I saw a picture of my dad when I was researching the Dover Demon, and it's freaking me out," he said. But she didn't understand, so he explained he'd been on his laptop researching the Dover Demon, a cryptid from Massachusetts, when he saw a picture of a man sitting in a chair alone in a dark room, "And there was a red circle next to his head and he looked exactly like my dad." For a moment, she had to admit, she felt the rumble of some panic, a horrible sense she was losing her grip on both of them at once. "Okay, show me this picture," she said. But when she saw it she laughed. The man in the photograph did look remarkably like her husband, but it was not her husband. "It's not your dad," she said. "Are you sure?" "I promise. It's a middle-aged white guy with a beard. They're everywhere. But look at this man's eyebrows. And his glasses are nothing like your dad's." "A person can get new glasses," he said, pushing up his own. So she started asking questions about the Dover Demon—lanky spider body, watermelon head—but when she tried to find out if something else was bothering him, something at school, with friends, he turned back into a stranger and asked her to leave his room.

The third part is shorter and it's the dream she had in the tent, which brought together the story her son had told, a memory from her own childhood, and the fact that that night, unbeknownst to them, a herd of cattle was out to pasture in a high flat field on the far side of those woods. She's back on the gravel spit. This is in California in 1985. She and her sister are sifting through gravel, looking for shells or river glass or bugs. They're alone. The river is slow-moving in summer and banked on either side by growth that's deeply green. At some point they hear cattle lowing on the opposite bank, behind the tangle of trees. They've grown up around animals and know the sound well enough, yet she can't remember ever finding it anything but unsettling. She's given this some thought and suspects it's because the sounds cows make are mostly the sounds of mothers trying to find their children or of children who've gone lost. Or else it was the library book she'd checked out in second grade, which claimed to relate the true story of a child who'd been frightened to death by a cow. Once upon a time in Oklahoma, a grazing cow approached an open window. Inside, a child was playing. The cow stuck her head between the gingham curtains. The child turned. The cow mooed. The child died of fright. But this was something else. This day on the river was something else. These cows sounded like they were being beaten to death. "Do you hear that?" she yelled to her sister. Her sister heard it too. Soon it got louder, closer. They kept expecting a herd of cattle to come crashing through the trees. Wherever they went on the gravel spit they could hear the awful lament, and sometimes they'd catch a word or two. Someone out there was shouting. Finally, they heard gunshots, and they stood on the gravel crying and whispering, "Stop it. Stop it. Stop it." Days later, the girls came across their parents speaking softly in the kitchen about a tragedy at a nearby ranch, but they never found out what had happened. She is holding a shard of bright-red river glass. There's something in the water. She knows it's bodies, and she knows there are forty-six, but she won't know if it's people or cows until—

Someone is screaming outside the tent. This is the fourth part. They wake in their sleeping bags, sweating, with socks laid over their eyes to block the light. "What time is it?" she whispers. Someone is screaming outside. "Probably just a meth head," her husband says, reaching for his watch. "*Just* a meth head?" says their son, and for a moment she thinks she might laugh. But someone is screaming, like speaking in tongues. She's never heard anything like it. "A quarter past midnight," her husband says. The screaming goes on and on. It's close, very loud. Possibly up at the bathrooms. She and her husband exchange a look. She's still half inside her dream—the image of a summer river hangs over all this like a veil. Then, the screaming stops. Her ears fill instead with the soft sounds of the woods, the singing of crickets and katydids, and also—is it?—from somewhere in the night comes the murmuring of cattle. "Do you hear that?" she whispers, confused. "What?" But a shadow falls over their tent—a lump of darkness, then arms, hands. "Who's there?" her husband shouts.

The fifth part should go here, but even as it's happening there's too much to hang onto: her husband, her son, that screaming, the cows, the heat, her ankle, the woods—

One night, when he was seven or eight, she read her son a story from a book called *These Bad Things*. It was surprisingly scary, and she knew she should stop, but they were so far in. She wanted to see how it ended. The main character was a rich man on his way to a famous museum. He saw many beautiful things there—marble busts, Egyptian reliefs, a Crusader's golden tomb—which eased his mind from his troubles, until it was time to go. Looking for an exit, he stepped into a gallery where a collage hung on the wall depicting people in rags, desperate people walking along a road, starving people, refugees, made out of oil and sand and clumps of garbage and teeth, and one kept drawing ladders, and one kept drawing sky, and one of them had a pipe for an arm, which extended out of the frame, into the room, and at the end of this pipe, as he walked by, was an envelope bearing the rich man's name in an unfamiliar script. The story had not been called "Your Name Here," but that's how she'd always remembered it. It isn't the rich man's terrible end she thinks of now, the message in the envelope, or what happened to drive those people down that long and desperate road, but the envelope itself, swinging in the room, and how she'd taken the time to imagine her own name written across it in some unfamiliar hand. She wonders why she did that. Would everybody do that? She's in the woods. Her foot is stuck. She turns her head away. A bad thing isn't a story, no matter what people say.

INSTALLATION

It's early when they arrive and no one else is on the river yet. *Glade coneflower. Rough blazing star.* She wades to a vague island and sets down her bag on the sand. To her left, the river, flowing at a clip, and to the right a still pool with a mild funk. Probably this is a sandbar, and not an island at all. Thinking a rhyme out of habit—vague, wave, vague, wave—she spots two day-flying moths and a butterfly in violent stripes drinking from wet sand. From the pool comes a definite clicking. It quickens, slows, disappears: *northern cricket frog.* Driving down at daybreak, her companion spoke of *chorus plants,* which exist inside a video game world he frequently inhabits. This plant, he explained, has tall stalks with purple flowers, and as it grows it creates a kind of soft melodic creaking. If you were lucky enough to find yourself in a *chorus plant forest,* the forest would be singing. The forest could grow infinitely, right up through the sky. Down here near the ground she hears the shushing of the river as it pushes past fallen branches, and even the sound the sand makes as it sparkles and suddenly crumbles under the weight of a bee. That butterfly, through her sunglasses, is distinctly blue and yellow. But she recognizes it as a *zebra swallowtail,* which means it's black and white. Then fifteen feet above her body comes the sound of a car unseen. Someone is driving to church down a nearby gravel drive. There's a book in her hands, but she does not read. At the line where water meets sand a thought is taking shape: Has this day happened before? These rocks around her are *chalcedony.* Like ordinary rocks grown over with some bulbous alien fuzz, a crystallized diamond fungus, glittering like snow set in opalescent glue. The Greek word "khalkedon" appears once in the book of Revelation, but it's a hapax legomenon, her companion said on the drive, a word found nowhere else, so there's no way to know if the gem in the Bible is the same as these sparkling rocks. She turns one with her toes. Only an inch under the surface the sand is cool to her touch. Now the river flashes light onto the undersides of leaves, which flap and wave on the many trees growing along its banks. *Wild plum. Black walnut. Shellbark hickory.* She has lost track of her companion. Did he walk upstream or down? She calls his name but her voice doesn't reach beyond the half-dam of fallen branches, while twenty feet above the sand comes the dreadful cry of a leaf blower in the hands of a disgruntled employee on one of the state park roads. She turns to scan the beach. Across from it, behind her back, a reddish bluff rises twenty feet. It's mostly overgrown with *invasive bush honeysuckle* and tangled native vines but here and there the bank goes bare, transformed into a sandy cliff punctuated by holes. The holes are bigger than her fist and smaller than a cat. The holes are veiled with webs, but she doesn't know that yet. She lies back on her towel, feeling completely alone. Is she reading her book or sleeping? What about the birds? In the car that morning she saw on her phone that scientists had created a new map of the universe: "Mind-Boggling 3D Map Shows 11 Billion Years." It's a map of a gap in time. Was it the idea of the boggling map in her hand or the actual road her companion was taking too fast through the woods that caused her to feel seasick? Something about moving through time like moving across a thought, or moving through a sentence like hurtling downstream. Down near her feet is the sound of two bees bumping the reddish sand. This river is called Big River. Presumably, at some point, the river is bigger than this. Then the butterfly flaps itself up the steep bank and lands on a pink globe of *phlox*. A large *swamp white oak* stands at the very top, and hovering near its uppermost leaf is the noise of a tractor in the field just beyond. She cannot see the field. She left her phone in the trunk of the car but it seems that hours have passed. Her companion, she assumes, will reappear for lunch. The fruit of the *chorus plant* is dangerous, he'd explained: it can teleport you anywhere, even inside a wall. It doesn't happen often, but if you teleport inside a wall you'll suffocate to death. A *mocha emerald dragonfly* appreciates the pool. The sun is overhead now. There's no shade on the sand. Without her having heard them approach, two canoes are passing. She stands on her island and calls: Have you seen my companion? Have you seen a man? But she cannot make out their answers. Don't something in the water! Connecticut in the water! the blond one seems to shout. Is she reading now? And what about the birds? *Bumblebee, hard at work.* That comes from a song. In fact, the songs of various birds are bouncing off the river, springing through her hair: *Louisiana waterthrush, yellow-breasted chat.* The day has gotten hot. Good thing she kept her lunch in her bag; her companion has not returned. But the noise of the *dog-day cicadas* rolls toward her, away, and back again in waves like visitations. He purposefully drove to a secret beach miles away from the lodge, miles from summer campers. She's alone at a beach in the woods. The woods are laced with prairie. *Sky blue aster. Sideoats grama. Little bluestem. Flowering spurge.*

Fast forward through the afternoon: three feet above her body now is the sound of her own ragged breathing, and far up in the open sky is the noise of a plane she can't hear. Are there fishes in this river? Are there *western mud snakes*? She works hard to keep herself upright in the current that feels like a pulse. She can touch the muddy bottom with her bag held overhead. The water is brown like chocolate milk but lit as from within, and hidden branches catch and scratch her legs. Rocks have filled her shoes. Of course you can't know what a virtual fruit will taste like, but her companion told her he imagines the *chorus plant fruit* tastes something like an apple. So a singing apple, she'd said. But why does she carry her bag? She could have stashed it in the bushes near her companion's locked car instead. When he parked the car this morning she saw a patch of *wild carrot* growing by the edge of the road: flat white face of a flower made up of many smaller flowers, like a galaxy in a swirl. She remembers now reading about the artist Yayoi Kusama, who when she was a girl hallucinated a field of flowers. All the heads of the flowers were dots and all the dots were talking. The field went on as far as the girl could see. The universe is dots, she recognized. A self-obliteration: she looked and looked and looked. Around a bend, near the shore, in an inlet where the current goes still, are tiny creatures skimming the surface, huddled close together, black and silver and round as little pills. The sun is in the west, bisected by a tree. Perhaps she should have waited at the beach? But a man pulled up in a truck and sat, and because she was raised in the country she does not trust a lone man in a truck. *Belted kingfishers* whiz and dive in the fast-moving water for fish. As the sun begins to sink, the scene on the river quiets. She pulls herself onto a sandy ledge and empties the rocks from her shoes. Her shoulders are lightly burned, the moon a pale hook in the sky. She listens to the river. Listening for her friend. Is he the one lost or is she? She remembers as a child never believing it was she who was lost the few times that she was. At dusk, new sounds emerge. High above is a *whip-poor-will* call, a *katydid* down by her knees. Suddenly a flashlight's beam appears on the opposite bank. Hello, she cries. Hello? She gets back in the water. But once across the river she finds a stranger in a T-shirt with letters spelling STAFF. Have you seen a man, she asks, with black hair, blue shorts? They lead her into the woods. Watch out, they finally say, there's a step going up, and it's a low door, so crouch a little; I will hold your bag. She crouches. She steps through the door. Something new is happening. She is standing on a platform now in absolute darkened space. Then, from under the platform, hundreds of fireflies rise. It's as if her body has activated the space. Soon she is conscious of cool dark animals moving all around her, animals moving nimbly and leaving silent tracks. It is a forest inside the woods. The forest extends from her body outward in all directions. How far does it go? It's a room-sized forest rectangle inside of which she turns. She turns again. She could reach out and touch the animals. Are they animals or animal structures? She could reach out and touch the trees or the dim projection of trees. A group of fireflies is called a light posse or a sparkle, or so her companion once said. The forest flickers, repeats: *white-tailed deer, shortleaf pine.* This forest is made out of stars. Now the fireflies seem to multiply and fill the darkened space; they no longer look like stars but like a net of lights. There are so many different kinds: forest light; harbor light; light between trees in a grove; cloud light; Martian light; alarm clock light; pink; the light at a European football game, or on a piece of bread; rainbow light; bomb light; laundered sheets; the sun; blinding light of a *daffodil;* the light from paper lanterns; cigarette light; LEDs; the light in a spiral stairwell; in murky waters; winter light, leaden-hearted; shredded lettuce light; light on a *copper iris;* light through a *damselfly* wing; *mute swans* on an opera stage; writing that's like the morning light, in every nook and cranny, in Mexico City, Tokyo; silver glitter; power stations; or the light from distant galaxies speeding through outer space. She sees a bench and sits, wondering what to do. Should she wait for her friend here? Then everything goes dark. A voice begins to speak, a professional narration:

There was once a woman named Anna who encountered the same grassy hillside every night at six o'clock. The hillside was modest in size, roughly ten feet by ten feet, and always deeply green. It didn't matter where she was, at home or in any busy downtown, somehow at six o'clock she saw that grassy field. In winter the hillside might be covered with snow, but she knew it was green underneath. In summer the light would linger on the grass. Sometimes the hillside surprised her, a sudden vibration of green out the corner of an eye. She often found the hillside distracting, especially when she was with other people who were unaware of its arrival. She might spot it while on a walk, nestled against the mountains, or out a hotel window crowding out some trees. Once she even saw it from the porthole of a ship: a lovely square of green against the gray-blue of the sea. What happens after you die? This was what the woman wanted to know. It occurred to her that this hillside was some kind of private gravesite, following her like a morbid dog wherever she went in the world. She wasn't exactly afraid, but then again she never approached it, even when there was time and she found herself alone. Most days she would continue to do whatever she'd been doing, and eventually, within an hour, the hillside would be gone. Then one evening the hillside appeared in her small semi-urban backyard, which was really more of a courtyard, with potted plants and several potted trees. It had appeared this way before. Usually the hillside was farther away, a city block at least, but it had happened like this once or twice before. The difference was that this night the hillside never left. It was there as she listened to the dire news. It was there as she took her bath. She could see it out her bedroom window. It seemed to vibrate, to glow—a trembling hyper-green site. She wanted to go to sleep. It was cool that night and there was a restlessness in her joints. When she got up to retrieve a blanket she saw the hillside was still there, and she had the unnerving sensation, a physical awareness, that all this had happened before. She knew she would open the door. She knew she would cross the courtyard in bare feet. Therefore she did both these things. She was now closer to the hillside than she had ever been in her life. Despite its relatively small stature, to stand in front of the hillside, she realized, was to stand in front of a complete environment, a unified vastness. It was made up of many individual blades of grass, each like a separate brushstroke on the canvas of the hillside—or the "hillside," as she began to think of it. The "hillside" evoked hillsides, she realized, but other things as well. It felt like a performance. It felt like an obsession in space. Was it real or was it a projection? What purpose did it serve? She was tired. Her feet were cold. She needed to lie down. That's when she decided to touch it. She let her hand drift down, palm first, and shut her eyes.

But even with her eyes closed her mind was as full of the hillside as the universe is filled with unnameable and namable things. *Rose mallow. Goldenrod. Blue wild indigo. Purple poppy mallow. Royal catchfly. Milkvetch. Compass plant. Water canna. River oats. Culver's root. Golden alexander.*

LOST LUNAR APOGEE

At dinner, a poet visiting from China said he planned, the following day, to try to get inside T. S. Eliot's childhood home. Someone else at the table, another man from China but who'd lived in St. Louis for years, told a story about being shown into that very house when he and his wife had been looking to buy. He hadn't realized where he was until he was inside it. He saw stairs for the family and stairs for the servants. "They wanted everything separate," he said. I knew only one person at the table. Like most of the others, she was a poet. It was cold in the cellar of the restaurant where we'd all met to celebrate the Chinese poet's visit, and out three small square windows, high up in the whitewashed wall, were plants shaped like coral but bright green. "It must have been a lot of work," the second man suddenly said into a bit of silence. I nodded with the others, though I had no idea what he meant. Then the waiter set down my wine. "Lunar Apogee," he announced. What a dippy name for a wine, I thought, as the woman to my right said it was the perfect title for a first book of poems destined to win awards. Was it the wine, then, that got us talking about Mina Loy— "Moreover," she wrote, "the Moon—"—and not T. S. Eliot's boyhood home? My friend claimed she'd seen Loy's hand-print on a sidewalk in Greenwich Village. Someone else said he'd visited her grave in Aspen. "She's everywhere," said the woman to my right, waving her bangled arms in the air as if Mina Loy herself might at any moment appear. Did I smile or laugh? The waiter set down a plate. Whenever I think of Loy, I said, taking my turn at the silence, I think of that ethe-real black-and-white photograph of her face—eyes closed, hair loose. Light breaks across her shoulder, and she turns herself into it ever so slightly. Then the visiting poet smiled at me, and I felt strangely unnerved. I could never be so un-self-conscious in a photograph, I said. "Die in the past, live in the future!" exclaimed the woman to my right. But isn't it ridiculous, I thought—I didn't say this part out loud; the conversation moved on without me—that after all the words of hers I've read—"The human cylinders / Revolving in the enervating dusk"—all those poems, when I think of Mina Loy I think of a pretty face? Of course thinking isn't looking, I went on, no doubt trying to justify my own superficiality, uneasy at having always been somewhat superficial in this way, but while my purest thought of Mina Loy might be an image of her face, that image is itself a kind of a thought. It is Mina Loy's face beset by or in some way accountable to certain words or ideas, which, in turn, bring further images with them: Mina Loy's face and the cover of *The Lost Lunar*

Baedeker (those long thermometer earrings); Loy's drawing of a figure shaking sky out of its hair; Joseph Cornell's *Portrait of Mina Loy* (she in a hat, smiling, atop a constellation); Mina Loy's face and those star-shaped lamps she made. It's no wonder she is celestial in my mind—ethereal, impossible. In a letter dated July 3, 1951, Cornell himself wrote to her to say: "I had a beautiful early morning in the back yard under the Chinese quince tree—very early, in fact not much after five; and I could not help but think of you, looking up at the moon—when the first rays of the sun turn its gold into silver." I felt sad then, suddenly forlorn, not sure why I'd spoken at all, and ridiculously middle-aged—no one had ever written me such a letter or ever would, sitting under a quince tree—sitting at that table with the handsome Chinese poet, thinking about a handprint on a sidewalk in New York. "It is not given to each of us / To be desired," wrote Mina Loy. I ordered a second glass of wine, a third. Now my problems were upon me, and I quietly seethed while stuffing myself with cracked Moroccan olives. The night was plainly doomed to spiral down. But an hour later, in a brightly lit gallery on Cherokee Street, the poet read his poems. After each, my friend read the English translation, and the poet sat to listen in the empty chair to my left. I felt a kind of intimacy with him then, though we never spoke, only smiled each time he sat, and especially near the end, side by side, listening to her read a poem in which a man whose wife has recently died sits alone at a table eating tangerines while inside his bookcase snow begins to fall.

On the drive home, snow began to fall. I passed an accident on Magnolia, another at McRee. It was in front of one of the old World's Fair mansions on Lindell Boulevard—the one that looks like a French château with wings—that under a streetlamp I saw her—"And 'Immortality' / mildews . . . / in the museums of the moon"—fur coat and gloves, snow in her long brown hair. There was no mistaking that face. I almost got into an accident myself, swerving hard to avoid a fox that streaked out from the park. My hands shook on the wheel. I had to pull over. The street was deserted. I blamed the wine, of course, cheapest on the list. I couldn't even bring myself to look in the rearview mirror. I'm driving home, I said out loud, as if to convince myself. So I did, my car to the curb, then hurrying up the path—I was stamping my rubber boots on the porch when the moon broke free from the clouds, landing on the fallen snow, the street asleep and alight: "the eye-white sky-light / white-light district." In the introduction to *The Lost Lunar Baedeker* we're told Loy named her book "not for the sun but for its ghost." Would we call the moon a ghost, or this a ghostly light? But I felt better, I did, turning my key in the lock, lucky to be home. Still, I couldn't stop shivering. Even my teeth felt cold. Here was the breakfast table strewn with the morning paper, there was my teacup, I passed through the hall—yet I was not soothed. Everything felt off, staged. It was like walking through a photograph instead of through a home. And though it was after midnight, I swear I could hear the babysitter upstairs reading to my kid, the story about a boy who finds a fallen star and is forced by his teacher to swallow it, then zooms into the sky. I felt a little dizzy on the landing. "An ocean of glittering blue-black waves," I heard the sitter say, "under a sky of huge galaxies." I touched the bedroom door. I stepped into the light. It was my child who was the first to scream, which is how you can be sure this story is true.

MY WONDERFUL DESCRIPTION OF FLOWERS

Last night my husband dreamed I left him, though my husband never dreams, or if he does he dreams of nothing—of sending an email, petting the cat. "I live not in dreams but in contemplation of a reality that is perhaps the future," Rilke, and not my husband, said. My husband brought up his dream over breakfast, but I had an early day, errands, a million meetings. I was almost out the door.

Later, on my way back home, I'm waiting for a westbound train, shifting a bag of groceries, when someone texts me a clip, so I tap my screen to watch. In it a man in a dark-blue suit steps up to a waiting group. His back is to the camera. He's speaking to a woman and a tall red-headed man—greeting them, or thanking them, or telling them good-bye. The clip is shaky, blurred. Someone made it by holding a phone in front of a TV screen. I can just make out the ticker; I catch "Iowa" and "White House." Then the man in the suit reaches out to touch the woman's arm. The woman steps away. I watch the clip again. It's not five seconds long. The man in the suit steps up to the group. He tries to touch her face. Not her arm, her face. The woman steps away. People are getting off the train. People are getting on. I have no idea who sent the clip. There's a number but no name.

Now comes a *coincidence*. There's a man on this train with a too-loud voice, a man in a dark-blue suit. At first he seems jolly, drunk. The westbound train goes "Haaaaaaaaaaa." He's friends with the whole world until he zeroes in on me. "Hello, wife," he says, taking steps in my direction. The train car lurches left. Then with a flash like a magic trick he produces a golden credit card and pops it in front of my face. He raises his eyebrows. Am I impressed? "This is my wife," he tells the train, but commuters stare out windows at the passing backs of mansions. The sun has nearly set. When we plunge into a tunnel he lifts that credit card up, high above my head. "The life breath of man is the lamp of the Lord," he says, his voice suddenly sonorous, his golden card a lantern now to guide us in the dark. Then the train comes to a stop. The doors slide open, but I don't move. But then I do, I run. I'm halfway out. I've timed it well. The doors are about to close. But the man in the suit is quick. His thinning hair and reek of booze. His hand is on my arm. "Hey," I say. But no one looks. I tear myself away. "Good-bye, wife," he calls. "I'll catch you another time."

Emerging from the station, I step inside the rain. I step into a cloud. All around, it smells like trees. Impossible not to picture a forest in the fog, but there's no forest here. I'm still holding the bag of groceries. I can still feel the palm of his hand. Then all the way up the hill to my house I assume he is inside—my actual husband, I mean, and I am his actual wife. Our child will be inside as well, no doubt on their computer, their bedroom window aglow. But when I arrive the windows are dark. I can't unlock the door. Then I unlock it and flip on the light. I call both their names up the stairs.

Two weeks before any of this, I stepped onto another train and smiled at a pale young man gripping the metal bar. This was the morning rush hour. There was nowhere else to stand. As soon as the doors slid shut, the young man started to talk. He never stopped, under his breath, just stared at my stomach, my dress: "So nice, so nice, so nice." Describing it later, I laughed, but my husband was not amused. "I'm not laughing," I told him, even though I was. A few days later I saw the young man again, I saw his picture, I mean, a shot from a doorbell camera, while scrolling the neighborhood app. He'd assaulted a woman not four blocks away, or tried to, on her porch steps, having followed her from the train.

Now I am home and my family is not. I leave my husband a voicemail. "Hey, where are you?" I ask.

For weeks my child has been obsessed with a video game called *Daphne*. In *Daphne* you're on an island. You're a man who has lost something, and you wander around the island muttering to yourself. The island is beset by mist. The mist sprouts seabirds, cliffs. Go left down a path to the ocean. Turn right through a doorway and descend a flight of stairs. There's something else there: moaning. From somewhere deep inside, the island is trying to speak. To get closer to the source, you enter a dark cave. The farther in you go, the more you're able to see; the walls of the cave are glowing blue with something alive or dead. You can just make out your booted feet. The moaning grows louder. Yet the first-person player's muttering can be heard above everything else, his footsteps on the rocky path, my child alone in their room. I hear it like a song at night: mutter, moan, and step.

But now their computer is sleeping. I shut their bedroom window. Then I go downstairs and open the door and call for the cat in the fog.

In a book I've been reading about an early twentieth-century painter, there's a passage halfway through about how she, the painter, Paula, liked to be alone: newly married, thus newly renamed, whenever her husband, Otto Moder-sohn, went away on a trip, she'd paint and paint and paint, and at whatever hour she liked she'd stop to eat and would not set the table. No candles. No meat. At dinner she'd read Goethe with rice pudding. "Half of me is still Paula Becker," she wrote, "and the other half is acting as if it were." But since I have to be on campus by eight, into the shining microwave I toss a frozen burrito. Then I text my husband: "I am not *leaving* I have to go to work."

The street lamps in the mist are wild pearls of light. I nod at a passing neighbor, walk down a half-hidden path. I cross a six-lane street. Next comes the row of campus garages wrapped with metal screens—everything is sculpture, maybe—which ripple and clink in the wind. Here is the staircase lined with dogwoods, which blossom-tunnels each spring, and then I pass the gates of the experimental prairie. I stop beside a bench. "Hello where are you?" I text. A plastic sign near the concrete path introduces the grasses by name. *Sideoats grama. Fowl Manna.* "The cluster of flowering heads," it says, "is called an inflorescence." Most of the plants come up to my chest, but here and there a thistle rises high above everything else, its bulbous purple head atop a thin green stalk. The tallest thistle brings to mind a camera, possibly alive, a sentient alien technology transmitting news of Earth. "Cursed is the ground because of you," God allegedly said. "Both thorns and thistles it shall grow." But I often feel like a thistle myself, a bulbous inflorescence, transmitting news of Earth.

Inside the lecture hall the walls are lined with latecomers who couldn't get a seat, and between these standing people are paintings from the eighties by a former professor's wife, the figures in them color-blocked and bent. The visiting writer is celebrated. Tens of thousands *follow* her. She takes a sip as people watch. Then she clears her throat. She places her glass on the lectern, but she sets it down in such a way that her face is inside the water. That is, from where I sit in the room, the water in the glass contains her entire face. Anyway, I think, they're probably back by now, with homework spread out on the table, and hopefully feeding the cat. "You need to get back to me please," I type, then set my phone to silent. The visitor begins. She is reading us a story about a woman on a trip. The woman has lost her glasses in a desolate public space. Now a stranger, a man, is offering to help. He leads her down a sidewalk. It's starting to get dark, but the two continue to walk. Someone beside me sneezes, but I quickly slip back in. The story is like a spell. There's a road, a woman, upheaval. They cross a grassy strip. Soon the man is telling the woman she has no one to trust but him.

Meanwhile the man in *Daphne* has probably killed his wife. That is the player's backstory, which you piece together from his muttered fragments as you wander across the island. "The man," my husband explained one night, "killed his wife drunk driving." "No," our child said, "it's that you asked another man to drive you home from a party, and it was that man who was drunk, and then there was a crash, but only Daphne died." Go left and you were the driver; turn right and you made a choice that caused your wife to die. Continue straight on the forking path and you'll approach a garden wall. It's a garden in the mist, a former garden, overgrown, and perched atop a cliff. But even within the garden walls you have to listen to his muttering, contemplate his regret. He is sorry, he is suffering, that much is perfectly clear. You pass driftwood crosses, orange poppies, clumps of yellow gorse. The sky is like a painting. You approach the edge of the cliff. "It's a graphic masterpiece," my child said, quoting an online review.

Something is waiting to happen, I think. This is just the lull.

What happens after a reading is called a *wine reception*. Mostly there is cheese. To my left a grad student persists:

". . . with Cate Blanchett and the interviewer says, 'Where do kindness and compassion exist, in your opinion,' and, like, 'Where do you locate a sense of a moral compass, in this brutal world, or whatever,' and Cate Blanchett says, 'It's in my vagina.'" My office is steps away, which means I can feign a reason, I can slip through the door and hide. Still, I hear their voices. I don't turn on the light. The window is black like beads of jet and I am the shape of a nightgown. I turn off my phone and turn it back on, but this produces no new texts, no emails, and no missed calls. So I rehearse what I've been told: I've been told that I worry too much. I've been told that I resist *trusting the signs* when things are going okay. But when are things ever okay? Bad things, I know, enormously bad, are happening all the time. And the little things add up, like my kid spending recess alone, again, eating alone at lunch, or how distracted my husband has been, how lately he shifts his face so that I'm kissing only his cheek, or how he keeps forgetting to bolt the back door even though he knows the doorknob lock is broken, so I'm regularly coming home to a house that's been unlocked, meaning anybody walking past might have stepped inside our kitchen, fingered the photos on our fridge, sneaked down into the basement—

A colleague calls my name. The crowd in the hallway has shrunk. The table is strewn with strawberry stems, and I have been invited: everyone is heading first to the train and then to a favorite bar.

"I'll walk as far as the fountains," I say, "but then I have to go home."

*

The bright lights from the stadium make the thick fog look like water, like a lake over our heads. I imagine I hear it lapping, but that's probably someone's shoe. As we pass two cops on bicycles, I stumble on the path, typing my husband an email, while a grad student is saying, "That thing you brought up in class," reaching out a steadying arm, "about not really having, like, one authentic voice." The fountains are just ahead, lit up in the dark, where the path beneath our feet branches out in three directions. I should take the path that leads to the road that leads to the hill to my house. But I stay with the group. I don't split off. I'm talking to my student, answering him with words. I let myself be pulled along, past the fountains with water like glass, into the station elevator, out onto the platform. As the eastbound train arrives with a hiss, I'm approaching my house in my mind: down the path, up the street, but all the windows are dark. I try it again and again—down the path, up the street—but nobody is home.

Four weeks ago this Sunday I was sitting in front of my laptop when a message popped up from a *friend*. He'd be passing through the city and did I want to get together in the early afternoon. "Sorry," I typed back. "I'm going to a pumpkin patch, if you can believe it, with a bunch of kids from my kid's school." I noticed then that this same person had messaged me over the summer, after I'd posted about being somewhere teaching a summer class. He'd gone to college in the area, he'd said. "It's my first time here," I'd written back. "Yes," I agreed, "it's beautiful." He mentioned the currents, the air, how good his body felt whenever he was there. The town was on the ocean and there were clumps of bright-pink sweet peas on the sides of all the roads. I'd forgotten this exchange, but now I remembered that, even then, I hadn't been able to place him. I'd only thought I recognized his name. I remembered now, too, how typing *sweet peas* had felt flirtatious, alone as I was in that other place, speaking privately with a man, though perhaps that feeling had more to do with how intensely I'd admired the flowers, and again I'd assumed he was someone I'd corresponded with before. But now I checked and he was not. I didn't seem to know him, and I was unsure how or why he thought that he knew me. Still, I figured, he must. Another message sounded. "Which pumpkin patch?" it said. I didn't respond. Minutes later: "Do you know where the pumpkin patch is?" Then: "Can you send directions?" "Sorry," I finally wrote, "I don't know where it is. I'm not driving." This was true. "I have to go," I said, and I shut my laptop and went downstairs and listened to the news. A billionaire was in outer space. The three hundredth mass shooting of the year had just occurred. An individual in Afghanistan had survived a drone attack.

Two hours later there was a knock on our front door. My husband and I were playing cards. "You get it," I said, and I stepped into the kitchen. How could I have known? Obviously, I couldn't. But I hadn't told my husband about the messages from that summer, or the ones that morning. What was there to tell? I heard the stranger say my name. I heard him say, "She knows me." I shook my head in the kitchen. My

husband asked him to wait. "It's fine," I said. "I'll talk to him."
"Who is this guy?" he said. "I don't really know," I answered.
I slipped on my shoes and stepped outside. The stranger was
alone on the porch. He looked at me like he knew me. He
smiled and looked away. I could sense my husband inside the
house, passing behind the walls.

But nothing bad happens in *Daphne*. It's always only lull.
No puzzle to solve, no objective, no end. There's only the
space of the player's despair—his constant talk, that muttering—and how you manage to feel, or where you manage to
go inside the landscape of his mood.

"I don't know him," I said, "I don't know why he came
here, I have no idea how he found our house." It sounded like
a lie, though it almost entirely wasn't. My husband went into
the yard to make sure that the stranger had gone, but even at
that moment there was a message on my phone. He could tell
I'd been happy to see him, he wrote, because I'd been so nice.
Another message would follow without a response from me,
and then another, and others, their tone increasingly hostile,
yet the officer we'd speak with would tell us there was nothing
the police could do without a *credible threat*. Then back there
in the moment a minivan pulled up. "Time to go," I called,
and my kid came bounding down the stairs pulling on their
jacket.

I've never been out this far.

When everyone else got off for the bar, I stayed where I
was, seated on the train. My students called out as the doors

shut, and I watched them slide away. I wasn't alone on the train. There were passengers seated or standing nearby, and the driver sat at the front. "This is an eastbound train," she said, and passengers got off, but nobody got on. When we finally emerged aboveground, the train was nearly empty. I watched the passing city lights and thought about the story that the visiting writer had read. The woman in it could hardly see. She was moving down the road, scared but also desperate, for all her own good reasons, moving toward something bad. But plot is so seductive. You don't really want it to stop. Or you don't know how to stop it. Then I realized the fog was gone. We were high up on a bridge, high above the river. Had the river swallowed the fog? But the river looked like nothing. It looked like empty space. Still, I knew it was down there, filled with fish and mud.

I'd emailed. I'd called. I'd texted so many times. When we cross this bridge, I thought, we'll be in a different state. Then we crossed the bridge. We passed a bright casino and a darkened RV park, then empty houses with missing bricks, then a house with missing bricks and a catalpa tree inside it. Then the train kept going, going and going and going through what seemed like more of nothing but must have been one enormous farm after another.

One afternoon last winter, my husband and child rode this train just to see where it ended. Despite the darkness, I can see now that it looks just as they described: a single track in a parking lot surrounded by fields of hay. There's one other passenger left on the train. I follow as she disembarks. She carries a sweatshirt, a purse. She seems to know where she's going. I follow her down the ramp. She pretends she doesn't see me, but I follow her all the way. I'm bad at talking to strangers, unless they ask for help. She doesn't ask for help or even turn around. She hurries toward a gray sedan, the only car in the lot. It reminds me of something I read once about a woman who couldn't sleep. She hadn't slept for weeks. One night she drove to a train station and parked in the empty lot. She sat inside her car. It was hard to tell, as a reader, if she had fallen asleep at last or not when her car began to shake. She dropped the keys by her feet in fear. Someone was outside her car, rocking it back and forth. Now the woman with the sweatshirt slams her door. She looks at me through the window. She starts the gray sedan. I watch her drive away. I cross the empty lot. At the line where the lot turns into the field, I take my phone out of my pocket. There's no service, which means no message, and the battery is low. It's a relief just to leave it on the ground.

In her film *The Beaches of Agnès*, almost at the start, Agnès Varda says to the camera that if we opened up people's bodies we would find landscapes inside. If you opened my body, she says, you would find beaches in me. Having crossed the field with its rolls of hay, then passed through a tangle of woods, I've come to some other place where the grass looks like a sea. The wind moves through the grasses, and I move through them too. At first the grasses come up to my knees, and then after a minute they rise as high as my head. Other things surround me too: star-shaped flowers in yellow and white, plastic netting, purple thistle, milkweed gone to seed. If you opened up my body, I think, this is what you'd find, exactly the place where I'm standing. There's a cross-rhythm from the crickets, plus the hum of distant traffic, plus the sound of drying grasses moving in the wind. My body's obscured by the waving of plants. This is the prairie at night. All you can see is darkness now and millions of flowers like stars.

Dresses

"It is not tiring to count dresses."
—GERTRUDE STEIN

SIXTY-SIX DRESSES I HAVE READ

1

This dress I am wearing in this black-and-white photograph, taken when I was two years old, was a yellow dress made of cotton poplin (a fabric with a slightly unsmooth texture first manufactured in the French town of Avignon and brought to England by the Huguenots, but I could not have known that at the time), and it was made for me by my mother.

2

"You are not a servant at the hall, of course. You are—" He stopped, ran his eye over my dress, which, as usual, was quite simple: a black merino cloak, a black beaver bonnet; neither of them half fine enough for a lady's-maid. He seemed puzzled to decide what I was; I helped him. "I am the governess."

3

A waiter passed her, followed by a sweetly scented woman in a fluttering dress of green chiffon whose mingled pattern of narcissuses, jonquils, and hyacinths was a reminder of pleasantly chill spring days.

4

Now your body fits perfectly into the square dress

5

And a funnier thing still was that now her coat was off she did look like a very intelligent monkey—who had even made that yellow silk dress out of scraped banana skins. And her amber ear-rings; they were like little dangling nuts.

6

after Mother
died her red
dress continued
baking pies

7

Her dress hangs on a door, the cloth is of a light background, revealing the surface with a landscape stained with the slightest of hue. Her portrait is not represented in a still photograph, nor in a painting. All along, you see her without actually seeing, actually having seen her. You do not see her yet.

8 & 9

They were both in white, and their dresses were rippling and fluttering as if they had just been blown back in after a short flight around the house.

10

Although her dress, her coiffure, and all the preparations for the ball had cost Kitty great trouble and consideration, at this moment she walked into the ballroom in her elaborate tulle dress over a pink slip as easily and simply as though all the rosettes and lace, all the minute details of her attire, had not cost her or her family a moment's attention, as though she had been born in that tulle and lace, with her hair done up high on her head, and a rose and two leaves on the top of it.

11

A few days before I exed out metaphors I was walking down the street in New York where I sometimes live. I was wearing this torn, floral dress, similar to something Janeane Garofalo would have worn maybe in *Reality Bites*. I was smoking a cigarette even though I said I had quit.

12

So home to dinner, where my wife having dressed herself in a silly dress of a blue petticoat uppermost, and a white satin waistcoat and white hood, though I think she did it because her gown is gone to the tailor's, did, together with my being hungry, which always makes me peevish, make me angry.

13

She could not face the whole horror—the pale yellow, idiotically old-fashioned silk dress with its long skirt and its high sleeves and its waist and all the things that looked so charming in the fashion book, but not on her, not among all these ordinary people. She felt like a dressmaker's dummy standing there, for young people to stick pins into.

14

I am writing to you, in your special writing dress made from scraps of lace as if it (the dress, the morning of writing ahead of you) is a café; as if, writing, you are hypnotizing not only the biologies of strangers and friends but also yourself. For this reason, when I think of you reading, I think of you as writing blindly. You read but you are also writing.

15

When they autopsied me,
I wore a white nightgown of malignant pearls
inside my body, as if I were a Queen that had swallowed my
    own crown
or a demented bride with her own cake sewn up inside.

16

: one second, a woman walks with a parasol in her hand, her dress white with small flowers : the next second, the flowers press against her skin, her back becomes the field of flowers, or the page of the exotic specimen of flora :

17

She sleeps in a red gown.
People around her are the size of rabbits and birds.

18

"How do you do? How do you do?" she murmured ceremoniously, and I was surprised to notice that she wore an ancient beautiful dress of green silk. But as she approached me I saw that her skin was dead white and glittered as if speckled with thousands of minute stars.

19

& then it was time to start the shoot we got called to set & the smoke machine was going on the faux dance floor & midway through the unremarkable song one of the goons tried to pull my sister's dress down in the front his finger actually touching her chest

20

The golden shimmer of Edna's satin gown spread in rich folds on either side of her. There was a soft fall of lace encircling her shoulders. It was the color of her skin, without the glow, the myriad living tints that one may sometimes discover in vibrant flesh. There was something in her attitude, in her whole appearance when she leaned her head against the high-backed chair and spread her arms, which suggested the regal woman, the one who rules, who looks on, who stands alone.

21

Pale purple shadows rest on the planes of her cheeks. Deep purple comes from her thick-shocked hair. Orange of the dress goes well with these.

22

The morning after, when the Navies were to fight, the Empress appear'd upon the face of the Waters, dress'd in her Imperial Robes, which were all of Diamonds and Carbuncles; in one hand she held a Buckler, made of one intire Carbuncle; and in the other hand a Spear of one intire Diamond; on her head she had a Cap of Diamonds, and just upon the top of the Crown, was a Starr made of the Starr-stone, mentioned heretofore; and a Half-Moon made of the same Stone, was placed on her forehead; all her other Garments were of several sorts of precious Jewels; and having given her Fish-men directions how to destroy the Enemies of her Native Country, she proceeded to effect her design.

23

She wore that day a pretty print dress that I had seen on her once before, ample in the skirt, tight in the bodice, short-sleeved, pink, checkered with darker pink, and, to complete the color scheme, she had painted her lips and was holding in her hollowed hands a beautiful, banal, Eden-red apple.

24

"I'll show you how," he said. Pressing my face to the floor, he ripped open my dress. There was a tearing sound, as if he had slit my back with a knife, and I tried to curl into a ball.

25

To be dressed like a man did not please, and would not suit

me. I had consented to take a man's name and part; as to his dress—*halte là!* No. I would keep my own dress; come what might.

26

And so by night the queen went from her palace,
Armed for the rites of Bacchus, in all the dress
Of frenzy, trailing vines for head-dress, deer-skin
Down the left side, and a spear over the shoulder.

27

I walk down the patterned garden-paths
In my stiff, brocaded gown.
With my powdered hair and jewelled fan,
I too am a rare
Pattern.

28

In our simple, cabin-like house I put on a dress that is deeply, deeply patterned with the night sky.

29

It is still night and I am walking towards the forest. I am wearing a long dress and thin slippers, so I walk with difficulty, following the man who is with me and holding up the skirt of my dress. It is white and beautiful and I don't wish to get it soiled. I follow him, sick with fear.

30

Part of my mind was listening to the quiet outside, part was staring appalled at him unfastening the buttons of my dress. Beginning from the top. One by one.

31

Lucian was disturbed by the milk that had leaked onto my dress: "What's that?" he asked. I sensed that it repelled him.

32

No, he wasn't cross: his daughter Norah was there, close by, perched among the branches now bereft of flowers, surrounded by the bitter smell of the tiny leaves; she was there in the dark, in her lime-green dress, at a safe distance from her father's phosphorescence.

33

By the mass! her breast-piece seems to me at this distance to be of rich coral, and her gown, instead of green stuff of Cuenza, is no less than a thirty-piled velvet! Besides, the trimming, I vow, is of satin! Do but observe her hands—instead of rings of jet, let me never thrive but they are of gold, aye, and of real gold, with pearls as white as a curd, every one of them worth an eye of one's head.

34

She came out, smiling, holding in front of herself a bright dress covered with suns. "You can't wear it in Paris," he said, and he saw her face change, as if he had darkened some idea she'd had of what she might be.

35

She felt she was choking in her blue velvet dress, with its high lace collar, its narrow sleeves, and a waist so tight that when she removed her belt her stomach jumped and twisted for half an hour while her organs fell back in place.

36

Elsbeth is flat against the plain. She is exactly the same height as the foxglove. The chickens are in front of her chest. The grass, the woods and the sky constitute three strips of colour. Her feet are in the roots. Her face is forever tilted towards childhood. Her dress is an explosion of white. Not a single shadow.

37

Her own dress was of the coarsest materials and the most sombre hue; with only that one ornament,—the scarlet letter,—which it was her doom to wear.

38

He looked magnificent as he came towards me. His resplendent, cherry-coloured Court cloak was lined with material of the most delightful hue and lustre; he wore dark, grape-coloured trousers, boldly splashed with designs of wisteria branches; his crimson under-robe was so glossy that it seemed to sparkle, while underneath one could make out layer upon layer of white and light violet robes.

39

R's impetuous proclamations about the passé significance of the patriarchy in contemporary times and her persistent sublimation of daily anxieties and sensory experiences through the subjectivity of her growing cat Kit-Ten, to whom she was incurably allergic, suggested a level of existence with which I was unfamiliar, and it was not until she appeared one night at a house reading in San Francisco wearing an orange dress and narrating the particulars of her recent femme self-awareness that I suddenly realized how we spoke not just a foreign language but the same foreign language, and how we had, unknowingly and seemingly without effort, become a "we."

40

She was sitting there with her hands folded in the lap of her dress, the Sears dress with flowers on it. There was a little mirror on the wall across from them, bright blue with the evening sky, and there were lace curtains behind them, and the chill of the window, and beyond that trees and fields and the wind.

41

Sooner or later she must be subdued into young-ladyhood; and it seemed befitting that the change should come gravely, rather than with the conventional polite uproar and fuss of "coming-out"—which odd term meant, as far as she could see, and when once the champagne bottles were emptied and the flimsy ball-dress lifted off the thin shoulders, going-in.

42

Margaret Kochamma climbed into the advertisement with her brown back-freckles and her arm-freckles and her flowered dress with legs underneath.

43

I used to dream about a dress that had the colours of the medicine wheel: black, white, yellow, and red. I finally made one from some clearance clothes I found at the Sally Ann: I ripped out the stitches down to the original panels, cut out pieces from a McCall's pattern I found at Value Village, and restitched them back into a dress that drapes over my body like a second skin.

44

With what can only be at Emily's request, an outside pocket, completely outside, a workman's pocket, was added to the right-hand side of the dress, level with the sleeve of the right hand. And no curator, no costume historian, can come up with a reason for that pocket to be there, if not to hold something the wearer used with regularity and wanted to be always near—could it have been something to write with, and a piece of paper?

45

Dark as midnight in her black dress, her haggard beauty and her unutterable woe.

46

They gave me a white dress. They know I am a barber and I didn't tell them I'm a barber. Won't. Can't. Boot in my throat, the food has to climb over it and then go down and meet with all their pals in the stomach. Hi sausage. Hi cabbage.

47

I have read that female prisoners to be hanged must wear rubber pants and a dress sewn shut around the knees because uterus and ovaries spill with the shock down the shaft.

48

She goes out. In her shortest dress, with her arms bare, her scalp bare, she wears no makeup. Her bald head feels cold when the wind comes by. She sits on a park bench.

49

When he unearthed an appropriately baroque dress (black lace on top, clingy polyester underneath), he took a picture of himself in that too, camera tilted down for the most flattering angle. He looked *good*, he thought. People should see these pictures.

50

Jesus glided out of the dark with underwater fluency; he was resplendent in a short crimson gown, a large velvet hat trimmed with lynx, a golden girdle around his waist, and a golden baldric trailing behind.

51

How magnificent her clothing is! The bird is on her gloved hand and is moving. She is looking at it and at the same time reaching into the bowl that the handmaid brings her, in order to give it something. Below, on the right, a little silken-haired dog is lying on the train of her dress; it is looking up and hoping that they will remember it.

52

Q. Gloria spent a certain amount for a new dress, a pair of shoes, and a purse. If the combined cost of the purse and shoes was $150 more than the cost of the dress, and the combined cost of the dress and purse was $127 less than twice the cost of the shoes, what is Gloria's real name?

53

The women lay on the bed and caressed each other. I felt amused, and gradually more and more excited. They danced round me. The girl naked under a transparent dress, and the woman, her breasts bared, cut open a melon, held grapes, sucked them, and rubbed herself on me, under me.

54

"Did I say blue—and slinky?" As Elizabeth nodded, Jessica continued. "It has a handkerchief hemline and—wait till you hear this, Lizzie—spaghetti straps and a neckline *so* low Todd will be panting."

55

She had clothed that thinness, Tatiana clearly recalled, in a very low-cut black dress, with a double layer of tulle over it, also black. This was the bearing and the clothing she desired, and she looked exactly the way she wanted to look, unquestionably.

56

A finger's worth of dark from daybreak, he steps
        into a red dress. A flame caught
                in a mirror the width of a coffin.

57

The salt pond is at work as soon as I'm awake
I listen to the rising sea architecture

I am wearing the salt dress
inside me

58

Everything about her shimmered and glimmered softly, as if her dress had been woven out of candle-beams.

59

Her dress, as she sat back again, spilled over both sides of her chair, in ample swelling folds, that reached right down to the floor. When Léon sometimes felt it under the sole of his boot, he stepped backwards, as if he had trodden on something living.

60

Micheline's dress was lace and silk and seemed to have been cut from time itself, so well suited was it for the ball and, Micheline fantasized, for her death bed.

61

Here, the texture and color in the sleeve of her dress meld into the pine boughs behind her.

62

"Yes, and her petticoat; I hope you saw her petticoat, six inches deep in mud, I am absolutely certain."

63

The morning road air was like a new dress.

64

"Why" "is she wearing" "a dress? What" "animal is she?"

65

I dance thinking of the plump lady, in her green crochet dress—the color of hope, they say—, in the pleasure she takes in dancing, replica or maybe a reflection of the pleasure she must feel while knitting; a vast dress for her vast body and the happiness to dream of the moment when she can show it off, dancing.

66

Must really lower my expenses, though there are days when one is sure that if one is better dressed, or more beautiful, in a kind of ceremonial dress if you will, one could get down to work.

* * * * *

1. Jamaica Kincaid, "Biography of a Dress"
2. Charlotte Brontë, *Jane Eyre*
3. Nella Larsen, *Passing*
4. Kim Hyesoon, "Orphan" (translated by Don Mee Choi)
5. Katherine Mansfield, "Bliss"
6. CAConrad, *The Book of Frank*
7. Theresa Hak Kyung Cha, *Dictee*
8 & 9. F. Scott Fitzgerald, *The Great Gatsby*
10. Leo Tolstoy, *Anna Karenina* (translated by Constance Garnett)
11. T Clutch Fleischmann, "House with Door"
12. Samuel Pepys, *The Diary of Samuel Pepys*, Vol. 8, 1667
13. Virginia Woolf, "The New Dress"
14. Bhanu Kapil, "Notes on Monsters: Section 2 (Wish)"
15. Joyelle McSweeney, *Dead Youth, or, The Leaks*
16. Mariko Nagai, *Irradiated Cities*
17. Mei-mei Berssenbrugge, "The Doll"
18. Leonora Carrington, "White Rabbits"
19. Khadijah Queen, *I'm So Fine: A List of Famous Men & What I Had On*
20. Kate Chopin, *The Awakening*
21. Jean Toomer, *Cane*
22. Margaret Cavendish, *The Description of a New World, Called the Blazing-World*
23. Vladimir Nabokov, *Lolita*
24. Yoko Ogawa, *Hotel Iris* (translated by Stephen Snyder)

25. Charlotte Brontë, *Villette*

26. Ovid, *Metamorphoses* (translated by Rolfe Humphries)

27. Amy Lowell, "Patterns"

28. Amina Cain, "Gentle Nights"

29. Jean Rhys, *Wide Sargasso Sea*

30. Anne Carson, "Just for the Thrill: An Essay on the Difference between Women and Men"

31. Celia Paul, *Self-Portrait*

32. Marie NDiaye, *Three Strong Women* (translated by John Fletcher)

33. Miguel de Cervantes, *Adventures of Don Quixote de La Mancha* (translated by Charles Jarvis, Esq.)

34. Mavis Gallant, "In Transit"

35. Isabel Allende, *The House of the Spirits* (translated by Magda Bolin)

36. Marie Darrieussecq, *Being Here Is Everything: The Life of Paula Modersohn-Becker* (translated by Penny Hueston)

37. Nathaniel Hawthorne, *The Scarlet Letter*

38. Sei Shōnagon, *The Pillow Book of Sei Shōnagon* (translated by Ivan Morris)

39. Pamela Lu, *Pamela: A Novel*

40. Marilynne Robinson, *Lila*

41. Sylvia Townsend Warner, *Lolly Willowes*

42. Arundhati Roy, *The God of Small Things*

43. Joshua Whitehead, *Jonny Appleseed*

44. Mary Ruefle, "My Emily Dickinson"

45. Henry James, *The Turn of the Screw*

46. Michael Ondaatje, *Coming Through Slaughter*

47. Rosmarie Waldrop, *Lawn of Excluded Middle*

48. Giada Scodellaro, *Some of Them Will Carry Me*

49. Andrea Lawlor, *Paul Takes the Form of a Mortal Girl*

50. Robert Glück, *Margery Kempe*

51. Rainer Maria Rilke, *The Notebooks of Malte Laurids Brigge* (translated by Stephen Mitchell)

52. Fran Ross, *Oreo*

53. Ann Quin, *Passages*

54. Francine Pascal, *Double Love: Sweet Valley High #1*

55. Marguerite Duras, *The Ravishing of Lol Stein* (translated by Richard Seaver)

56. Ocean Vuong, "Trojan"

57. Kim Hyesoon, "The Salt Dress Inside Me" (translated by Don Mee Choi)

58. Edith Wharton, *The Age of Innocence*

59. Gustave Flaubert, *Madame Bovary* (translated by Geoffrey Wall)

60. Fleur Jaeggy, *Sweet Days of Discipline* (translated by Tim Parks)

61. Akiko Busch, *How to Disappear: Notes on Invisibility in a Time of Transparency*

62. Jane Austen, *Pride and Prejudice*

63. Zora Neale Hurston, *Their Eyes Were Watching God*

64. Alice Notley, *The Descent of Alette*

65. Luisa Valenzuela, "Tango" (translated by Frank Thomas Smith)

66. Alix Cléo Roubaud, *Alix's Journal* (translated by Jan Steyn)

Art

"Translation is amazing, because it presumes that there is something that needs to be carried from one place to another. But where is that thing?"

—RENEE GLADMAN

Ostensibly I write novels and stories, yet I often find myself more interested in spaces and things than in plots. The world is astonishing. I want to ask: How might fiction be conceived of as a space within which we attend to the world? A way of opening spaces—prairies, paragraphs, rooms—in which the world can occur? How might a story embody a specific way of looking? By looking I mean seeing, but I also mean a way of being in relation to the world, a politics of attention.

Take Georges Perec's novel *Life: A User's Manual,* which unfolds as one long radical act of attention. "Question your tea-spoons!" he says. Or Piotr Szewc's *Annihilation,* which takes the reader step by step through a tiny town in Poland—its people, butterflies, buildings, streets—before the Holocaust comes to erase it. Or Renee Gladman's *Calamities.* Or Lydia Davis's *The Cows.* Or Virginia Woolf's "Kew Gardens." I had a student several years ago say he thought "Kew Gardens" was boring because it was just like being in a garden. First of all, he's wrong, it's not like that, it's an experience in language. But if he were right, if a story was *just like being in a garden,* wouldn't that be amazing?

I've always liked this line: "A *picture* held us captive. And we could not get outside it, for it lay in our language and language seemed to repeat it to us inexorably." Wittgenstein was talking about a picture in the mind, whereas I am interested in pictures in the world. He was thinking about a mental picture formed by language, and I am thinking about language formed by an actual picture. Yet the idea of being captured in an image and in language, in an image in our language—how a story could be a story and also be a garden—is just what I want to try to articulate about so-called ekphrastic writing, or writing in response to visual art.

In his essay "Art as Device," the Russian formalist critic Viktor Shklovsky argues that we perpetually grow habituated to everything around us—"Habituation devours work, clothes, furniture, one's wife, and the fear of war . . ."—and that the job of art is to make the world strange so that we might see it again rather than simply recognizing it out of habit. The way art does this is through a process he calls остранение, transliterated as "ostranenie" and translated as "defamiliarization" or, neologistically, as "enstrangement" (i.e., enchantment + estrangement). "Art exists that one may recover the sensation of life," he writes, "it exists to make one feel things, to make the stone *stony.*"

Perhaps I write fiction in response to visual art not only to foreground a practice of looking but also because my encounters with visual art frequently make the world strange, and it is when the world is strange, or when I am awake to its strangeness, that I am most compelled to write.

I used to work at a publishing house that specialized in translations of experimental fiction. A conversation that seemed always in the air there had to do with various ideas about how translation should work. One idea I found compelling was that a translation should try to create, as much as possible, *the experience* of what it would be like to read the original work. You can imagine this gets complicated when a book is formally challenging, has been written to upset easy assimilation. How do you render an experience of strangeness without causing the reader to assume that the peculiarities are in the quality of the translation rather than in—or also in—the original work? Yet what an impoverishment it would be for Anglophone readers not to have translators willing and able to capture in English the formal strangeness of Cristina Rivera Garza's stories, for example, or the poems of Kim Hyesoon. I don't mean the original is preserved in some pure or perfect state. It's not a replicator I'm talking about, but a pulling through of strangeness into strangeness.

It seems to me that ekphrastic writing, at least the kind I'm interested in, takes place as a dialectic between these two impulses, between art's ability to *make strange* what has grown familiar and translation's desire to *make recognizable* the experience of one artwork inside the space of another.

When I first saw Laura Letinsky's still lifes in her book *Hardly More Than Ever,* it was as if I was standing inside those rooms instead of where I sat. Then I returned to the room I was in and the world around me was altered. It all went *whoosh.* Then, abruptly, *blam.* You might even call it an ecstatic experience: I'd been placed outside myself. In fact, the etymology of "ekphrasis"—where the Greek *ek* = "out" and *phrazein* = "tell"—seems to encourage the possibility for ecstatic utterance, for speaking outside the self.

I've seen Letinsky's still life photographs referred to as "domestic arrangements," "elegant voyeurism," "rampant with indelible delicacy and indirect debauchery," "a landscape of leftovers floating weightless around a room." They are formally impeccable. They seem to glow. Fruit and flowers and crystal and silver. They boast a pretty palette Letinsky has called "acid meets pastel." Yet these photographs are much more than simply pretty. They buzz. There's an odd plasticity to them. Everything seems about to collapse. Life itself feels staged and the stuff of life half rotten.

First published in 2011, my novel-of-the-suburbs, *SPRAWL*, was written with Letinsky's still life photography in mind and, through it, toward still life as a visual and political form—all wrapped up, as it is—as is suburbia, historically—in the display-nature of bourgeois culture. The narrator, a housewife, stalks her neighborhood, her home, hyper-attuned to all that she sees:

> There's a new addiction local women negotiate in different ways, on separate blocks, in pantsuits and bathrobes, in houses and public spaces. It's concealed between stones and transferred from neighbor to neighbor via gossip. I involve myself in it like anyone else. Or maybe I just think about it. Anyway, the book says lemon and orange juices have medicinal properties. It shows sweet and sour citrus fruits together on one page. Other fruit is admired for its geometrical construction (apple, melon, cucumber, etc.). I am completely interested in plates of fruit, or fruit baskets, or baskets of fruits and flowers. I have theories of arrangement I share with Mrs. Way and Mrs. Daniels when they arrive. I set out one basket

of peaches and grapes, and then I set out a plate with peaches, grapes, apricots, and roses. In the window facing the street is a large vase of flowers (carnations, irises, tulips, bluebells), and one sea-shell, and a bowl of candy, and a cricket. These displays are in a state of perpetual readiness. Moonlight pours in the open window. The mixture of consumerism and eroticism is particularly commented on. For dessert I serve cherries and strawberries in dark china bowls on a white tablecloth with hard precision.

But what *counts* as ekphrasis, my students want to know. So we start with a series of definitions, spanning centuries, and I love the comparisons, I love etymologies, though that stuffy air of permanence always makes me want to push back. *Merriam-Webster,* for example, defines ekphrasis as: "a literary description of or commentary on a visual work of art." *Oxford English* as: "the use of detailed description of a work of visual art as a literary device." Both are standard (and certainly preferable to the *OED*'s 1814 "florid effeminacies of style"), yet many of the most interesting works of ekphrasis I've come across—I mean in fiction specifically[1]— don't *describe* an artwork at all, or not in any conventional sense.

---

1 Most critical writing on ekphrasis focuses on poetry. I'm interested in how these same ideas apply to fiction, and in what other ekphrastic possibilities narrative prose might open up.

See Eley Williams's "Smote, or When I Find I Cannot Kiss You in Front of a Print by Bridget Riley." In this story, the narrator is at a museum with someone she desperately wants to kiss. We know the narrator and her date are standing in front of Bridget Riley's vertiginous black-and-white "Movement in Squares" because the story tells us so. I could talk about how Riley's painting already looks like a stylized kiss, a coming together of forms, or how Williams's text is laid out with clauses that break from their paragraphs, snaking black letters across and down the white page. But what fascinates me is the real print hanging on the fictional wall. Williams has opened a fictional space inside of which the Riley exists. She's hung it up for us to see. Then, rather than *describe* it for us, Williams endeavors to capture something of the spatial, aesthetic, transformative visual experience of the Riley and to pull that into her prose. Her story, therefore, reproduces not the print but the experience of the print's particular formal strangeness. As the narrator stands in the gallery and spirals into a cacophony of indecision in front of the dizzying image, the reader encounters a riot of slippery black-and-white prose: "I could have, rather than grown anxious and aware of the attendant, dreamt of dressing you in coats trimmed with lemur tails and corner you in fields filled and frilled with Friesian cows and badgers' scalps and California king snakes." The story goes on in this way, dizzying the reader with its busy sentences of black-and-white imagery, creating a vertiginous intensity that is very like the Riley, but all its own. Against the assumption of ekphrasis as writing in service to visual art, all the energy headed in one direction, here we have something more like a conversation. We might even say that Williams's story operates as a diptych with Riley's print: the two pieces together throw their energy back and forth.[2]

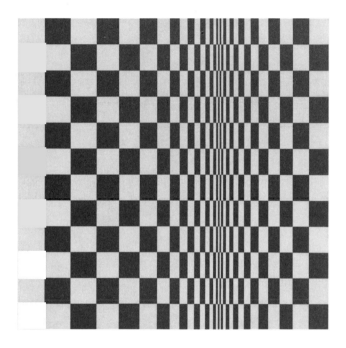

In *A Horse at Night*, Amina Cain talks about seeing artist Bill Viola's work at a museum in Chicago; she writes: "Some

---

2 For more on the energy of a diptych, see Eric Dean Wilson's essay "Regarding Diptychs."

years after, I saw a video clip by Viola on YouTube, *I Do Not Know What It Is I Am Like* (1986), the one of the owl toward which the camera gets closer and closer, until the camera person (Viola?) is reflected in the owl's eyes. The video is very short, barely three minutes, and it is not a story, or even story-like, yet there is something in it I'd like to do too, in a story."

Lydia Davis has called this relationship "analogy." In "The Impetus Was Delight: A Response by Analogy to the Work of Joseph Cornell," she writes a prose that sounds less like the recognizable prose of Lydia Davis than the language—if it were language—of a Joseph Cornell box:

> the invited guests are customers of the carpet cleaning company, those who have had their carpets excellently cleaned by them during the past year, they come into the house shyly, it is always unusual but it is especially beautiful at Christmastime, because of all the Christmas decorations and the special arrangements of the mother, who has fashioned little snowy scenes involving miniature fir trees and figures skating in circles on glass lakes, penguins or little men and women, who do not stop going round and round while the guests walk through and pause to sit at a table and talk and eat cake . . .

Because it isn't only the guileless brilliance of the "little snowy scenes" that brings to mind Cornell. Look at all those clauses! Each phrase is its own small box (within the larger box of the paragraph, each paragraph a box within the larger box of the piece) into which something precious has been placed for us to see.

In *Picture Theory,* W.J.T. Mitchell expresses a skeptical position: "Ekphrastic poems[3] speak to, for, or about works of visual art in the way that texts in general speak about anything else. There is nothing to distinguish grammatically a description of a painting from a description of a kumquat or a baseball game." He says: "When vases talk, they speak our language." Yet it's exactly the vase's language that interests

3 Let's read "texts" for "poems."

me. What is the energy or the syntax *of the vase*? In my favorite ekphrastic writing, the voice of the vase is there. Call it an ecstatic translation. Or analogy. I know that in writing *SPRAWL* I listened hard to the syntax of Letinsky's images—their angles, their flatness, taxonomies and light—letting my work be formed (or deformed) by the photographs, not trying to overcome the "obstacle" of translation but hoping to be changed by the effort.

Someone once asked me if *SPRAWL* could be read as an oblique but elaborate review of Letinsky's work. I don't see it that way. But John Keene's "Acrobatique" offers one of the best examples of ekphrasis-as-commentary that I know.[4] Keene's story is about Anna Olga Albertina Brown, a.k.a. Miss La La, a nineteenth-century acrobat and the real-life subject of Edgar Degas's 1879 painting *Miss La La at the Cirque Fernando*. The historical Miss La La was an aerialist nightly hoisted into the circus's elaborate domed ceiling via a rope, with a mouthpiece clenched between her teeth. In Degas's painting, Miss La La is high up, not so much foregrounded against that ceiling as part of it: still, embellished, stuck. We cannot see her face. We see her brown skin, her black hair. What happens as she steps from the painting to the text is that Miss La La, the object of Degas's painting and his gaze, becomes in Keene's story the speaking subject. No longer an objectified body but a person with a voice, she tells us, for example: "last fall because of an

---

4 See also Tisa Bryant's collection *Unexplained Presence*.

extra-heavy flow and no time to get back to my rooms I had to stuff any gloves I could find into my tights and only Kaira knew, and we prayed like Catholic girls to the saints that there would be no accident." This Miss La La is fully aware that they call her *la Venus noire*. This Miss La La has a family, a menstrual cycle, ambitions, childhood memories, friendship, hard dislikes: "as I was heading back into our dressing room another man drew forward, bent down, gray threading his beard, his large, lidded eyes hard at me like lead shot, he introduced himself as *M. Edgar Degas*." The story reclaims the woman behind the faceless body in the painting, and Keene does this, at least in part, by giving her back her eyes.

We open with a description of the domed circus ceiling from her singular vantage point: she hears the audience calling, their words flying past her "up into the rafters, scattering among the trusses, vaulted arches, the cupola, clambering amid the bats and the blackbirds, across the brickwork seen only by its masons and ghosts, though I see it . . . that map of bricks and buttresses and plasterwork of this chocolate jewel box." It is a description of the painting as only Miss La La can offer, as a character inside its fiction, *from within*. The story ends, breathtakingly, high above the crowd. Miss La La catches sight of M. Degas below, sketching, trying to capture her on his page, but no, she tells us, no: "I elude him and all of them, gliding higher, toward the freedom of the dome." She sees it all.

Nothing about Keene's story advertises its connection to the painting, and then again nothing hides it. When I've taught this story, most students have been surprised, after reading it, to learn of its relation to the Degas. Is *this* ekphrasis? they want to know. When you bring the two together, suddenly the story is something else. Suddenly the painting is subject. I ask them: Did Keene see something in the painting that wasn't there? And is it possible to look at Miss La La now without hearing the voice of Anna Olga Albertina Brown?

Maybe I don't think of *SPRAWL* as commentary because, despite the fact that I hadn't met Letinsky when I wrote it, the book has always had, for me, an air of collaboration about it, similar to what I described between the Williams and the Riley: two forms meeting, a kiss. Is that how a translator feels? As I was writing *SPRAWL*, I felt deeply connected to Letinsky's work, so much so that whenever I lost momentum or confidence, her project or vision could re-invigorate my own. At times, I've gone so far as to describe my relation to her photographs as one of ownership—not in the sense of having bought them and brought them home, but a more fundamental feeling that they somehow belong to me.

In 2007, a Frenchwoman named Rindy Sam kissed a white Cy Twombly canvas—part of a monochromatic triptych—on display at the Museum of Contemporary Art in Avignon. "I just gave it a kiss," she said. "I thought the artist would understand." According to the BBC, restorers have tried "30 products" to get out the stain. The *New York Times* says Sam was wearing "Bourjois's true red satin Rouge Best" when she kissed it. The owner of the Twombly sued for the painting's full multimillion dollar value. One art blogger wrote: "There are enormous questions at stake here!" Should the museum replace one white canvas with another white canvas? Would that second canvas *be* a Twombly? What if Twombly handed it over? Had Sam in fact brought value to the work? Coincidentally, her trial came days after a break-in at the Musée d'Orsay in Paris during which a group of vandals punched a hole through a Claude Monet scene of sailboats on a glittering Seine, the water like a mirror of the sky. That kiss was "as aggressive as a punch," argued the plaintiff's lawyer. "It was an act of love," Sam said. "I wasn't thinking." "Don't think, but look!" Wittgenstein wrote. "I do not share the same vision of love," rejoined the lawyer. "For me love requires the consent of both sides." But a painting can't give consent. She wasn't kissing Cy Twombly. Does it change anything to know that Sam considers herself an artist? "The artist," she has said, "left this white for me."

After I wrote *SPRAWL,* I worried Letinsky would hate it. My hands shook as I packaged a finished copy to send her. Of course I hadn't left a mark on her actual work. Or had I? And what exactly did Sam mean when she said she thought the artist would understand?

Or take Nathalie Léger's *Suite for Barbara Loden* in which Léger, a French writer and archivist, tells a story about herself and her mother via an investigation into the life of the American actress and filmmaker Barbara Loden and, in particular, Loden's 1970 film *Wanda.* Loden, meanwhile, based *Wanda* on a real-life woman she'd read about in the newspaper, a woman who abandoned her family and hooked up with a drifter who convinced her to help him rob a bank. *Suite for Barbara Loden* is like an infinity mirror of women in pain and seeking. There are two main narrative arcs. One is the story of Léger trying to understand Loden (and her own mother) via research into Loden's life and work. The other is the plot of the film. It's *Wanda.* Huge swaths of the book are simply the film unfolding: "And so Wanda is killing time in a shopping mall; walking slowly, she stops in front of a shop window, examines the mannequins' white plastic bodies posed between huge bouquets of yellow and orange flowers . . ." The eye of the book is an eye that watches the film. The reader watches too. The book is not like a screenplay, but it is, in parts, like a film. They say an ekphrastic text can never actually bring the image before you, yet to watch *Wanda* after reading *Suite for Barbara Loden* is a fascinating thing. You watch for the first time what it seems you've already seen.

The book received awards and praise in French and in its English translation, but on Amazon you could once find this blistering one-star review: "In 'Suite for Barbara Loden,' Leger [sic] claims filmmaker Frederick Wiseman 'quite calmly' advised when she couldn't get facts, 'Make it up. All you have to do is make it up.' As a journalist and Barbara Loden's sister, Susan Loden, I am offended and repulsed that this recommendation was apparently followed in what should be presented as a work of fiction. Leger [sic] offers unattributed and apparently plagerized [sic] material that has not been fact checked and or lifted from a novel. Beyond that, there is an inordinate quantity of BS fantasy and opinion."

Is it a novel? An essay? Is it documentary, criticism, or art? Richard Brody in *The New Yorker* said: "Here, now, is a remarkable new book that does everything—biography, criticism, film history, memoir, and even fiction, all at once." But the reaction of Loden's sister underscores a concern. What are the ethics of ekphrasis? Does it matter what Degas might have made of "Acrobatique"? What Letinsky might make of *SPRAWL*? I tell my students that Keene's story is both its own work and a new point in the painting's life. Or it is its own work and a new point in the story of Miss La La. The text does not erase the painting. The two can exist together, throwing their energy back and forth.

And yet, when it comes to collaboration, the scholars seem to agree that ekphrasis *isn't*. It isn't collaboration because the image isn't there, and it wouldn't be ekphrasis if it were. "Unlike encounters of verbal and visual representation in 'mixed arts' such as illustrated books," writes Mitchell, "the ekphrastic encounter in language is purely figurative." But sometimes encounters are messy. Take Ben Lerner's "The Polish Rider," a story about a painter who, the night before a gallery opening, accidentally leaves two paintings in an Uber. This painter, Sonia, and her friend, our narrator—a writer—race around New York City trying to find the lost work. As their goal becomes increasingly unlikely, the narrator thinks about "recuperating the lost paintings through prose." In perhaps the ultimate example of what I might call metafictional ekphrasis, the narrator tells the reader his plan: he's going to write something—this story!—to present at the gallery in place of the missing work.

Lerner's story does a beautiful job of conjuring Sonia's paintings:

> Every painting in Sonia's show depicted the same thing: the famous kiss between Erich Honecker, the leader of the German Democratic Republic from

1971 until the fall of the Berlin Wall, and Leonid Brezhnev, the head of the U.S.S.R. from 1964 to 1982 . . . The canvases were, as always with Sonia's work, meticulously composed, but each was composed in a different historical style. One canvas depicted the kiss abstracted into Cubist shapes and volumes, another was Caravaggesque in its chiaroscuro (the kiss of Judas?), another involved a mixture of verisimilitude and blur that recalled Gerhard Richter, and so on.

It's textbook ekphrasis, figurative, but the story is also doing this other stranger thing, working to *recuperate* the lost images with the text in our hands. To replace paintings with language? To make text and image one? But here's where it really gets messy, because after "The Polish Rider" was published, the real-life painter on whom Lerner had based the character of Sonia, Anna Ostoya, decided to paint the paintings Lerner had described in the story, paintings he'd imagined based on her earlier work. So Ostoya's work inspired the paintings in his story, then the story inspired new paintings—a.k.a. reverse ekphrasis—and meanwhile he writes a second story, "Late Art," in which the protagonist, again a writer, decides to write a story about his painter-friend Anna, who lost two paintings in an Uber. To further complicate all of this, both "Late Art" and "The Polish Rider" can now be found accompanied by a range of Ostoya's paintings in an embossed hardback—an illustrated book!—with the same name as the original story, which is also, incidentally, the name of a seventeenth-century portrait by Rembrandt in which a man sits astride a horse in crimson cap and tights.

In *The Polish Rider* (the book, not the painting) the conversation between forms is accessible as a conversation—a collaboration—because it was one, it became one. Yet, if it's direct, it isn't simple. There is always a silence at the center of this kiss, a peculiar moment when the paintings turn us back to the writing or the writing to the paintings with something left unsaid. In other words, while they use each other, point toward each other, neither form depends on the other, and for this reason the Ostoya-Lerner image-text collaboration strikes me as particularly successful. It's slippery. Meanwhile, even while existing in the pages of an image-text collaboration, Lerner's writing remains essentially ekphrastic. The whole book engages ekphrasis in a traditional sense, but it's also *about* ekphrasis, with a capacious sense of what ekphrasis in fiction might be. In "Late Art" Lerner writes of his writer: "For several years he had been obsessed with the relationship between fiction and the other arts, had started to think of fiction as a curatorial form, a medium in which you could stage encounters with other media, real or imagined."

Fiction as gallery, a space of installation—the real print on the fictional wall. So this is one way to think of ekphrasis in fiction. And there's also crawling inside the picture to see out from eyes within. And there's that other way, too, that weird alchemical transfer, like when Amina Cain says she wants to do in language what Bill Viola does with the owl. She doesn't mean she wants to describe Viola's video or place it in her story, but to write a story that captures something Viola's video captures—some narrative effect, feeling, an experience of form. What would that story be like, I wonder, the one that gets closer and closer until at some point the thing being looked at sees the looker back?

My own chance at image-text collaboration came about when the artist Richard Kraft asked me to write pieces to accompany a series of collages. While living in Berlin, his wife, Lisa, had come across a Cold War-era Polish comic book—*Kapitan Kloss*, about a spy who infiltrates the Nazis—and had passed it on to Richard, who was now in the process of exploding it, taking its panels of heroic-looking World War II officers (plus Nazi scum) and mixing in images of rabbits and birds, the Amar Chitra Katha comics of Hindu mythology, vintage soft-core porn, language from children's primers, etc. Richard wanted texts that would run parallel to the subversive non-narrative of his collages, related yet interruptive, to further explode the already anarchic impulse of his work. We began with a long phone call, during which we decided that, per the model of John Cage and Merce Cunningham—Richard is co-editor of Cage's delightful *Diary: How to Improve the World (You Will Only Make Matters Worse)*—ours would be a relationship of non-subordination. After that conversation, we simply wouldn't talk.

Cunningham's collaborative performances could come together almost as the curtain was about to rise, the lighting, music, costumes, and choreography having been worked on separately and often in isolation. It is collaboration as collage, elevating juxtaposition and chance over unity of effect. Cunningham has said:

> John Cage didn't like the idea of one art supporting another or one art depending on another. He liked the idea of independence and wondered if there were another way we could work separately to produce a work of music and dance. The first things we made were short solos, and it was difficult for me to do, not having the music as support in the tradi-

tional way. But at the same time there was marvelous excitement in this way of working, so I pursued it.

In the beginning, writing the pieces for what became *Here Comes Kitty* was marvelously exciting. It was bizarre. It felt like I was writing ekphrastically but with my eyes closed. There was a visual work somewhere in the world and I was trying to tune myself to it, only I hadn't seen it yet. Like a translator translating what is only just being written? For a time I wrote toward what Richard—a British-Indian Jew— had told me—a Jewish-American WASP—about disrupting *Kapitan Kloss*. He said: "What if the Nazis say things they'd never say?—like 'I am a big girl! I sing! I sing!'" I wrote toward Cage and constraint, toward Cunningham and the idea of abstract dance. In the absence of the actual image, I was trying to capture something of Richard's process, something in the nature of collage itself:

> I'd seen her face on a bird, years ago. Now there she stood, proud as day, staring at my son. Was she thinking of a bird—red devil—flitting through the hall? "What I'm talking about here is local," one of the women explained. "Egg yolks, peanut butter, even commercial cheese!" Another woman, totally oblivious: "Skipping is not recommended." So this was the major change. I don't mean pink blossoms or some rabbits on the lawn. I was lactating. Lactating! Together we watched the news: "Indian Martian MOM

LAYS AN EGG with her Latest Egg—NOT Big Enough." Yet what could I do but stand there and steam? What could I do but go on wearing that silly mustache for all the world to see? Then "Ha!" he said, my little son. He rocked back on the carpet. He grabbed his penis, little soothsayer, and said: "It starts with a woman. She goes to a shop. There's something weird there. Poop! Something happens to her: she dies. Something happier happens: there's a new woman who saves the woman who died. The women go and see the Statue of Liberty. It looks like a butterfly. They go to a huge island made of poop and they step in the poop and it makes their feet turn into monster feet. They sit and relax in the water. They are monsters forevermore." Was I ashamed? Blithe spirit! I stood and smoothed my dress.

In *The Play and Place of Criticism,* Murray Krieger writes that the ekphrastic text "must convert the transparency of its verbal medium into the physical solidity of the medium of the spatial arts." Earlier, I said that I write fiction in response to visual art because the process foregrounds looking and because visual art helps estrange the world for me, but I think it also has to do with the obvious physical solidity of visual art, and the fact that a text is also inherently, if less obviously, solid: physical, spatial, plastic. Imagine a story as a physical experience, like an installation we move through. A hole we drop inside of. Or like a painting we apprehend only after the reading is done. Krieger's notion of the ekphrastic text "converting" itself, bending itself toward the physical—the Davis toward the Cornell, the Williams toward the Riley—gets closest, out of everything I've read, to describing the peculiar energy of the visual object's power to bend and warp my prose. With *SPRAWL* I was trying to capture the energy of the absent-present image as if I were a camera. Click. With *Here Comes Kitty* I didn't have the image at first, but the reader always would. How should that change what I'd do? What sort of image-text relationship would result? So I worked, not with answers, but inside the space of these questions, and with the generative model of collaboration I find in writing with eyes open and with other artists and other forms in mind.

DANIELLE DUTTON

106

IMAGES

1. Whitney Hubbs, *Untitled (Hair),* 2013. Courtesy the artist.
2. Roni Horn, *Untitled, No. 4,* 1998. Iris-printed photographs, 2 parts. 56 x 56 cm / 22 x 22 inches © Roni Horn. Courtesy the artist and Hauser & Wirth.
3. Laura Letinsky, Polaroid, 4 x 5 inches, from "Times Assignation," 2010. Courtesy the artist.
4. Bridget Riley, *Movement in Squares,* 1961. Tempera on hardboard 123.2 x 121.2 cm 48 1/2 x 47 3/4 in © Bridget Riley 2021. All rights reserved.
5. Peter Bruegel the Elder, *The Hunters in the Snow,* 1565. Oil on panel, 117 cm x 162 cm. Kunsthistorisches Museum, Vienna.
6. Hilaire-Germaine-Edgar Degas, *Miss La La at the Cirque Fernando.* National Gallery, London.
7. Unidentified artist, *Miss La La,* c. 1880. Albumen silver print on paper. Image Collection, Zimmerli Art Museum at Rutgers University. Museum purchase 1999.0187. Photo: Peter Jacobs.
8. Rembradt van Rijn, *The Polish Rider,* ca. 1655. Copyright The Frick Collection.
9. Detail from *Here Comes Kitty: A Comic Opera* by Richard Kraft with interpolations by Danielle Dutton, Siglio Press, 2015.

WORKS REFERENCED

Brody, Richard. "Barbara Loden: 'A Woman Telling Her Own Story through the Story of Another Woman.'" *The New Yorker* (online), November 1, 2016.

Brown, Carolyn, Merce Cunningham, Laura Kuhn, Joseph V. Melillo, Thecla Schiphorst, and David Vaughan. "Four Key Discoveries: Merce Cunningham Dance Company at Fifty." Panel Discussion, Brooklyn Academy of Music, Brooklyn, NY, October 18, 2003.

Bryant, Tisa. *Unexplained Presence*. Providence: Leon Works, 2007.

Cage, John. *Diary: How to Improve the World (You Will Only Make Matters Worse)*. Eds. Joe Biel and Richard Kraft. New York: Siglio, 2019.

Cain, Amina. *A Horse at Night: On Writing*. St. Louis: Dorothy, a publishing project, 2022.

Davis, Lydia. *The Cows*. Louisville: Sarabande Books, 2011.

_____. "The Impetus Was Delight: A Response by Analogy to the Work of Joseph Cornell," in *Essays One*. New York: Farrar, Straus and Giroux, 2019.

Dutton, Danielle. *SPRAWL*. Seattle: Wave Books, 2018.

Gladman, Renee. *Calamities*. Seattle: Wave Books, 2016.

Léger, Nathalie. *Suite for Barbara Loden*. Translators Natasha Lehrer and Cécile Menon. St. Louis: Dorothy, a publishing project, 2016.

Lerner, Ben and Anna Ostoya. *The Polish Rider*. London: MACK, 2018.

Letinsky, Laura. *Hardly More Than Ever: Photographs 1997–2004*. Chicago: The Renaissance Society, 2004.

Keene, John. "Acrobatique," in *Counternarratives*. New York: New Directions, 2015.

Kraft, Richard with interpolations by Danielle Dutton. *Here Comes Kitty: A Comic Opera.* Los Angeles: Siglio Press, 2015.

Krieger, Murray. *The Play and Place of Criticism.* Baltimore: The Johns Hopkins University Press, 1967.

Marshall, Alexandra. "The Human Stain." *The New York Times Magazine* (online). December 23, 2007.

Mitchell, W. J. T. *Picture Theory: Essays on Verbal and Visual Representation.* Chicago: University of Chicago Press, 1995.

Perec, Georges. *Life: A User's Manual.* Translator David Bellos. Boston: David R. Godine, 1987.

____. "Approaches to What?" in *Species of Spaces and Other Pieces.* Translator John Sturrock. New York: Penguin Putnam Inc., 1997.

Shklovsky, Viktor. "Art as Device," in *Theory of Prose.* Translator Benjamin Sher. Normal, IL: Dalkey Archive Press, 1991.

Szewc, Piotr. *Annihilation.* Translator Ewa Hryniewicz-Yarbrough. Normal, IL: Dalkey Archive Press, 1999.

Williams, Eley. "Smote, or When I Find I Cannot Kiss You in Front of a Print by Bridget Riley." *The White Review*, Online Exclusive, April 2015.

Wilson, Eric Dean. "Regarding Diptychs," *The American Reader* (accessed online), September, 2014.

Wittgenstein, Ludwig. *Philosophical Investigations, second ed.* Translator G.E.M. Anscombe. Eds. Anscombe and Rush Rhees. Oxford: Basil Blackwell, 1958.

Woolf, Virginia. "Kew Gardens," in *The Complete Shorter Fiction of Virginia Woolf.* Ed. Susan Dick. San Diego: Harcourt Brace Jovanovich, 1985.

"Woman Fined for Kissing Painting," BBC.com. November 16, 2007. http://news.bbc.co.uk/2/hi/entertainment/7098707.stm.

Other

Among many reflections in Thomas De Quincey's essay "The Last Days of Immanuel Kant," the reader is offered a glimpse at the philosopher's bedtime routine. Kant had a strict habit, it turns out, of reading by candlelight until ten o'clock, whereupon he would remove his mind from exertion for one golden half hour, sure that a mind laden with study would be prone to wakefulness, and so he simply sat. Until, at last, he would undress, lie down, and wrap himself in a blanket—cotton in summer, wool in autumn, then, as the air cooled, both of these together. Once Königsberg was in the fullest grip of winter, frost felling ancient oaks and small hills of snow on every pitched rooftop, he'd sensibly switch to eiderdown or, to hit the nail on the head, to a blanket of eiderdown ingeniously stuffed, in its upper third, with wool instead of feathers (a blanket, then, both padded and stuffed), with which he'd enfold his body—nesting more than covering, we're told. Here's how: first, he'd sit on the side of the bed and with an agile motion vault obliquely into his lair; next, he drew one corner of the bedclothes under his left shoulder, and, passing it below his back, brought it round so as to rest under his right shoulder; fourthly, by a particular *tour d'adresse,* he operated on the opposite corner in similar fashion, finally contriving to roll the blanket around his entire person. How pleasing it is to imagine Immanuel Kant thus enswathed (self-involved as a silkworm) as Thomas De Quincey stands close at hand, snuffing the candle or checking that the curtains are shut against the cold, and taking notes, mentally if not literally—noting, for example, how the author of *Critique of Pure Reason,* once nested, would often exclaim, "Is it possible to conceive of a human being with more perfect health than myself?" Yet you would be wrong in imagining things this way. For the truth of "The Last Days of Immanuel Kant" by Thomas De Quincey is that not much of it is, in fact, by Thomas De Quincey. The *truth,* which hides not behind lies but behind De Quincey's curious relationship to quotation and citation, is that this intimate description of Kant's bedtime routine comes from Ehregott Andreas Wasianski's 1804 *Immanuel Kant in seinen letzten Lebensjahren,* which De Quincey translated and annotated in such a way as to leave the reader with the impression that the words and experiences were De Quincey's very own. And so it is Wasianski, not De Quincey, snuffing Kant's candle, Wasianski, not De Quincey, with the presence of mind to inform us that when hosting a party, rather than keep a bottle of decanted wine with a servant, Kant, *anacreontically,* preferred to keep one at the elbow of every single guest. Who Wasianski was is not of great importance (a friend, a priest, a musical inventor) because it is De Quincey whom we think of as we read. "It is Thomas De Quincey that history remembers," I say to my companion sitting opposite on this bullet train as we look out at the landscape whizzing by.

Looking at a rainbow shooting straight up from a field, I recall an interview with the Belgian writer Jean-Philippe Toussaint, who when asked what made his books funny answered: work, work, work. "Yet I can't help thinking," I tell my new friend, "that the humor I find in 'The Last Days of Immanuel Kant' is at least partly accidental." Or perhaps that's me eating straight out of its hand? Take the section in which De Quincey explains that Kant is not popular here and now (the here and now in question being nineteenth-century England) because he cannot be, and he cannot be because he wrote in German, and because of what, in German, he wrote. He wrote: All of the elements of the manifold of i (where i is some arbitrary intuition) are such that H is or can become conscious, in thought, that all of those elements, taken together, are accompanied by the *I think*. I think, announces De Quincey—in the middle of a tremendously long footnote printed in an exceptionally tiny font, yet offered with total conviction, as though these are the final words on a man and his body of work—*popular* the transcendental philosophy can never be.

Thus we have an essay written and not-written by Thomas De Quincey about a philosopher whose philosophy, the essay's writer-slash-not-writer tells us, cannot be liked, or not liked by many, and yet, he goes on, any thinking person *must* be interested in Kant the man. A great man, he argues, though in an unpopular path, will always be an object of liberal curiosity—and, indeed, there is ample evidence with which to back him up! From Diogenes Laërtius to our very own here and now, we seem to long to know just how the great man eats his breakfast (in Kant's case oatmeal, promptly at five each morning), how he takes his exercise (a walk after dinner each night, alone, so as not to be bothered with conversation, talk forcing one to take in air through the mouth, whereas Kant preferred to take in air through his nostrils, ensuring the air reaching his lungs would arrive in a state of less rawness, especially in winter, the nose being an instrument of warming), how he sleeps (enswathed!), and, above all, how he dies. Like all great men, Kant died without any sweat. Only his eye was rigid, writes Wasianski, writes De Quincey, and his face and lips became discolored by a cadaverous pallor—and that was all. No crying or pleading, no vomit or piss. Unlike the rest of us, a great man looks out at the abyss and simply exhales. Or so we are told. And so we can hold it in our hands. This small old book in bright-green leather—*The Works of Thomas De Quincey: Last Days of Immanuel Kant and Other Writings*—and I hold it up to show my neighbor as our train plunges into the dark.

"De Quincey," I say as we reengage the daylight, "is best known as an opium eater. In fact, we are told, he was a visionary at six." His earliest memories were dreams. When his sister Jane died aged three, the younger Thomas assumed she'd pop back with the spring rains, like a bulb. When his sister Elizabeth died aged nine, he stood beside her corpse and fell into a trance. Thus Thomas took leave of his youth: a school, a tutor, a tutor, a school. Some called him weak and effeminate, others gifted and premature. Throughout his life De Quincey would be troubled by pain in his guts. A brilliant student, fluent in Greek, in 1802 he ran away from Manchester Grammar, tossing his trunk down the stairs one moonless night. Of course the lives of the Romantics were filled with desperate flights, but De Quincey was perhaps the most adept at sleeping in actual fields and trudging through mountainous rain. A smallish teenager, he calls the sunset pompous. He watches the girls in bonnets. Then he is found and disappears again to befriend a virgin whore in London's soggy streets. At last he arrives at Worcester College, Oxford—but he'll run away from that school, too, calling it *Ancient Mother.*

"You might," I say, seeing a skeptical sort of spasm pass over my companion's face, "be inclined to think I inject so much moisture into this story because of the drops now pelting our window, and so be more likely to doubt the truth of what I say. But the fact is that the first forty years of the nineteenth century saw excessive rainfall in England. Truly there were those who called it 'outstandingly wet.'"

"Interestingly," I continue as the horn blasts and we barrel past a cow, "for all the care with which De Quincey recounts Wasianski's account of Kant, the great man to whom he was truly devoted was William Wordsworth." He called himself, at seventeen, *zealously attached,* then went to live for a decade in Mr. Wordsworth's beloved Dove Cottage, its tangle of ivy and scallop-pink walls, where he irritated the elder poet's more fastidious nature. It's such a shame to meet the ones we worship. De Quincey would later advise: Never describe Wordsworth as equal in pride to Lucifer: no; but, if you have occasion to write a life of Lucifer, set down that by possibility, in respect to pride, he might be some type of Wordsworth.

Eventually, he settled in Edinburgh with his wife and chowder of kids. As regards the De Quincey children: three boys died, one gruesomely, one in China, and Sara Coleridge accused the father of neglecting them all and worse. Yet, he was silver-tongued, even or especially in his insults. That no one in England read Kant was a sign, he was sure, of the nation's intellectual emasculation; Goethe was no good; Coleridge was a thief. Incendiary was De Quincey, always catching his hair on fire, his haystacks of papers too. When he died at seventy-four a semblance of youth came over his face. He looked, we're told, a boy of fourteen. "Thank you," he said, then simply expired. They called him a gracious corpse.

Now from the window of this speeding train I see hill after hill after hill after hill and all their grasses blurring. Incidentally, the writer I've been most recently reading on De Quincey—in an essay called "Thomas De Quincey"—was also the translator into Italian of *Gli ultimi giorni di Immanuel Kant.* "And so," I tell my drowsy companion, for indeed it seems this train will never stop its oscillation, never meet an ocean, never approach a mountain it can't pass, "the writers begin to blur like the grassy hills!" That writer-translator's name is Fleur Jaeggy. Born in Switzerland and educated by nuns, there were horses and she rode them speaking Italian, German, and French. Later she modeled for pictures but found it dull. Known for being private, she lives in Milan with frescoes on her walls. I came to her work through her fourth book, a slender novel in which, as in the life of its author, a Swiss girl is sent to be educated in a boarding school managed by nuns. The school is in the Appenzell where the writer Robert Walser died while walking one Christmas Day. Someone had the sense to snap a picture of the body: hat just out of reach, final line of footsteps caught forever in the snow. It is as if, having met his fate on the path, Mr. Walser simply agreed.

When people mention that Jaeggy translated De Quincey, they invariably cite as evidence "The Last Days of Immanuel of Kant." Has ever a translator—I mean here De Quincey—so eclipsed the one he translates—I mean now Wasianski? Emerson wrote: Do not go where the path leads, go instead where there is no path and leave a trail. How interesting then to go where the path goes and leave a trail nevertheless. For her part Fleur Jaeggy still lives, so there is nothing yet to say about her death. At times it feels like all the stories that need to be written are written, and all the lives that need to be lived have been lived.

Several of her friends were writers too, and they talked about the body. Where is the body when you write? You are always writing from the body, they said. But we can't really feel the body in your work. We don't believe in the bodies in your stories. Your stories are all words. Bring the body into your writing, they said.

She wasn't sure.

When she was writing she was in her body, she couldn't argue with that. But how to explain that she was somewhere else as well? When she was writing it was as if she were working from six inches above and in front of her own head. If the energy of writing fell back into her body, all writing stopped. Then she was just herself, sitting in a chair. She was ready to admit—to herself, if not to her friends—that keeping that energy afloat was peculiar work, bodily work. It was like bathing a squirming baby that you weren't allowed to look at. Babies are so slippery. You can't believe it the first time you bathe a newborn. It's like trying to wash the water.

Writing was like that. Like water. More like water than like a body. Wasn't that something she liked about it? Then again, if her friends were able to simply sit in their bodies and write, maybe this meant that their writing was more connected to the world, the real world, which everyone seemed to want. Everyone wanted more of the real, more of the world. Maybe it meant that they could get up from their writing and go do something else, immediately, something useful, wash a baby in real life, for example, looking at the baby the whole time. They might even wear those gloves made out of washcloths, little pastel mitts, which made it so that the baby would never slip from their grasp. They could soap the baby's back without any worry that they might drop the baby out of its blue plastic tub and into the dirty kitchen sink. They wouldn't have to worry about the baby's little arm or leg slipping into the garbage disposal, oh god, or about the baby sliding out of their ungloved hands and onto the bathroom floor, cracking its head, the blood, oh god. Not that she had a baby. Not that any of her friends had babies. This isn't a real baby, she thought. What was a baby in a story? It was a word. The word was baby. The word was body. Was her own body a word? She couldn't stop thinking about it all the way home: body, body, body, body, body, body, body.

The following day, as she was walking to the grocery store, an acorn fell from a tree, bounced off the sidewalk, and hit her on the nipple. Hit her squarely on the left nipple. But was squarely the right word? Was nipple? Was acorn? It hit her hard too. Hard, certainly, even if not squarely.

"Doubt equals writing."

That's Marguerite Duras in her essay "Writing."

I could write something called "Not Writing." I am writing it. Soon, I'll have been the one who wrote it.

Whenever I'm not writing, which is most of the time, what is it I'm doing? I am someone pursuing *fitness*. I am obviously sometimes sleeping. I am someone collecting the sentences she reads: "The question of food is salt. The question of food is salt. The question of food is salt."

That is Clarice Lispector.

Of course it's natural for a writer to not be writing, even most of the time. What can be surprising is the extent to which one might feel, upon finding oneself newly not writing, struck—as if one has dropped the reins and fallen. As if a moment before one was up on a horse and now one is down on the ground. All one can say, looking around, is that one is not a one upon a horse.

Meanwhile, K and S are collaborating on tone. C just

sold a book. R is giving a series of lectures on drawing and language and lines. Last night in a lecture, she said: "I am writing and by writing I am moving and by moving I am living."

By not writing am I not moving and by not moving am I dead?

Sometimes, when not writing, I'm listening to the news. I might even cry in the kitchen. I'll weep while stirring the soup. I'm of no help to anyone when I cry. Do I help anyone when I write, or when I am waiting to write? Tonight I make the soup and I surround the soup with anguish. The whole world is anguish, except the soup.

A while back, at his request, I wrote texts to accompany the images in an artist's book of collages. An assignment minimizes doubt, that's true. Yet was I happy writing? Later, he asked where I find the things I want to use in my work, and I said: "Visual art has always been one of the main places I go." I told him how I'd been looking at Agnes Martin's paintings and also reading her texts, and that reading her writing about painting made me want to write stories.

He said: "Agnes Martin's writings are amazing, I agree with you there. But what really happens as you read them? How does what you've read manifest in what you write?"

And I said: "Well, I'm reading this essay about how her paintings are 'about' nothing, yet when you look at them there's an obvious beauty and a kind of performance happening—something *happens* to you as you look at them. I read that and look at her work and I feel that performance and I think, yes, that's exactly what I want to do, *exactly* what I want to make happen with language."

The problem is I've chosen words, which can't seem to be about nothing. Words don't make things happen—performances or feelings—without also making meaning.

miserable means wretchedly unhappy

friendless means alone

ugly can be hideous or plain

For some reason, lately, I can't stop telling people about the time my sixth grade teacher asked me (miserable, friendless, ugly) to stand up and show the class that I didn't have a typically Jewish face. In an interview, the artist Moyra Davey says that shame is beautiful when we bring it out in the open. I wonder if we have to do anything to our shame other than share it. Shape it?

"They came, these restrained, reserved, exquisite paintings, as visions, for which she would wait sometimes for weeks on end, rocking in her chair . . . 'I paint with my back to the world,' she declared."

That's Olivia Laing in "Agnes Martin: The Artist Mystic Who Disappeared into the Desert." Of Martin's paintings Laing writes: "They aren't made to be read, but are there to be responded to."

Is it wrong to want to write toward what isn't intended to be read? What I want is a story that's an object that can turn itself inside out. So perhaps what I'm thinking of as inspiration is something else instead. Not to be writing like Martin but to be *not writing* like her.

I look again at one of R's drawings, the one that hangs on my wall. She describes her drawings as language with its skin pulled back. In a second evening lecture, R says, "Fiction is a category of not-knowing." And it's true I want a story to be a hole I drop inside of. Then I fall asleep. While sleeping I have one of those dreams in which you think you're awake in your bed. In this particular iteration of that category of dream, there's a ladybug on my sheets. But the ladybug is enormous, at least as big as my head, and it's reared up on its hind legs as if ready to attack. I cry out, "Marty, there's a bug!" And Marty gets rid of the bug. Then I remember that I left a bright-green poisonous snake over on my bookshelf. So Marty grabs the snake behind its head and takes it into the yard. Then I remember that I left something else on my bookshelf, something worse, on the shelf below the snake, but Marty's still outside. I know I have to handle this myself. I walk slowly across the room. What's there is an enormous gray pulsating slug. It's gelatinous, repulsive. It fills the entire shelf. There are many smaller gray slugs attached to the larger slug, and they're feeding off it somehow, making sucking sounds. As they suck, the smaller slugs seem to be constructing sacs around themselves, dark hard sacs like scabs. The whole thing is magnetic, revolting. But these words don't come to me in the dream. In the dream there is only the slug, filling the shelf, and the certain knowledge I have that it is a thing I have made.

In the morning, over oatmeal, I tell my son about the dream, which he finds completely hilarious. Yet the moment

I've spoken it aloud, I experience a kind of electric shock in which I understand that the slug in the dream is the very thing I've been hoping to write, which is *not writing*. And it isn't about doubt at all. It's this whole new thing, unseen in the world, replacing the books on my shelf.

That afternoon, in an email, K asks if I'm thinking of writing about Agnes Martin. I don't know how to tell her about this thing I've already done. "I have been wanting to write about an old woman," I say back.

Now I'm in bed re-reading a favorite novel in which the main character, a polite spinster aunt named Laura, abruptly leaves her life in London against the wishes of her family and moves to a remote country village to be alone. Tramping through meadows, she decides to become a witch. She listens to the violets, listens to the trees. One day, she runs into Satan in the woods. They have a lengthy conversation. Near the end of this talk, a bug lands on Laura's arm and she smacks it. "Dead!" Satan says, and the word spreads out in ripples like a rock dropped in a pond.

SOMEHOW

Somehow, they were swimming in the canals. Later this part seemed hazy, but somehow they were all there: Lila, her little boy, and James, a former student. Whether James had arrived with Lila and her son or was simply also there enjoying the day was unclear, but at some point it became clear that they were there together.

It was an industrial landscape but a popular place to swim, so close to the city, with shops and cheap bars on the wharf above. Lila was conscious of having on her shabbiest swimsuit: matching her skin tone, a one piece. It was no longer as elastic as it had been when she bought it, yet strangely smaller too. Her breasts were barely covered by the fabric, which did not seem to her remotely attractive. She kept checking to make sure her nipples were not exposed. Impossible to say what James was thinking. She was hardly tuned in to his thoughts. He was only there, somehow, in a way he'd not been before. Her little boy was a fine swimmer. Little eel. His little-boy skin glistening in the light. He laughed and laughed and James laughed with him. She watched them from a distance. A french fry floated past. She'd started her period that morning and wondered if when she got out of the water the crotch of her suit would be red. Her tits felt huge, misshapen even. James looked over and smiled. It was like wearing a suit made of plastic wrap, everything pressed down and on display.

A few weeks earlier, before the semester ended, Lila had gone to hear a famous Buddhist give a talk. The lecture was in the city but at a Buddhist center in a large and wild-seeming park, large enough and wild enough, anyway, that when she got to its center, where the wood-and-glass lecture hall stood, it seemed she'd somehow managed to get outside the city. The air felt cool. She stopped in some shade beside a clump of purple flowers. Forest bathing, she thought. Had she heard that on a podcast? Inside the hall the famous Buddhist cleared his throat. Weirdly, he began by telling a story about Laurie Anderson going to hear a different famous Buddhist give a talk in a different city, where apparently she pledged to be kind for the rest of her life. Weird because Lila had just been reading about Laurie Anderson, that she was NASA's first ever artist-in-residence. Was Laurie Anderson in outer space? It turned out she'd just visited some labs. In a lab in California, she wrote in her red notebook: There will one day be a staircase up to Mars. Certain of the researchers were unimpressed. "What's she going to do, write a poem?" one said. Anyway, the story went that after she pledged to be kind for the rest of her life, Laurie Anderson panicked. Unsure whether she was upset because she'd promised too little or because she'd promised too much, she approached one of the Tibetan monks and asked him out for coffee. The monk said yes and sat down to the first espresso of his life. He sipped and listened and then he began to talk, faster than he'd ever talked before, saying, essentially, knock it off. He said the mind is like a wild white horse. Or he said her mind was like a wild white horse. Lila wasn't sure. The woman beside her was coughing horribly. Was Laurie Anderson's mind like a wild white horse, or was everyone's? Was her mind—was Lila's—a wild white horse too?

When it was time to go, James asked for a ride. They tossed wet towels and shoes into the trunk of her car. Lila's boy was four. On the drive he told them he was a dog, that he'd been a dog all along, ever since he was born. "You're a funny guy," said James. "I'm not a funny guy, I'm a dog," he said. James laughed. His teeth were very white. "Where should I drop you?" she asked. The hairs on her arms were stiff from the salt in the canals. But James said he could easily walk from her place. He'd been to her apartment before, she remembered, with several other grad students after a lecture downtown. The speaker had been a Polish writer who described his poems as torsos without heads. It snowed and she'd given them coffee. Now it was summer and the city was steaming. She'd thrown a pair of denim shorts over her ill-fitting suit.

All three outside the apartment door, Lila offered James water—what else was there to do? He stood in the kitchen drinking as she went to rinse her son and put him down for a nap before returning to the bathroom to rinse the salt off herself. The apartment was spare: a kitchen, a bathroom, her son's room painted blue. No vacancy, she thought, peeling off her suit. Of course there was another room, her own, down the hall, where she stood in two wet towels, one around her body, one around her hair, as James came in and took off his clothes and laid down on the bed. Almost instantly she thought of an essay by Eileen Myles. It was an essay about a painter named George whose former student comes into the room and takes off all his clothes and lies down on the bed. It's quiet in the room, but thousands of sounds fly around outside. A "luminous back" she remembers reading. George paints from memories. But can you pull the noise of the world apart and say *that's* a cicada, *that's* a plane, that's two people kissing upstairs? Then there was that dream about a different former student, a graduate student in geology who wrote a poem about erosion. "There are no perfect circles in geology," it began. In the dream she'd followed that student to a salmon-colored hotel, pushed him against a wall like she'd seen people do in movies. But is it in the same essay that Myles admits seeing the Taj Mahal in person is a total disappointment? I paint, George says, because I like to paint. In one painting a woman serves a man a bowl of soup. Between his fingers are fingers, between his thighs her hand. Between his lips she sees his teeth as white as paper and remembers the famous Buddhist calling a sheet of paper the sun. A piece of paper is a cloud, then the rain. It is the tree and the logger and the logger's mother too. And if you look hard enough you'll see yourself on the page—tits heavy, fingers spread, waiting for something to happen. Isn't that what they'd written? Isn't that what they'd meant? Wait, stop. That was a different one. That was a different one. That was a whole other essay.

A DOUBLE ROOM

There's an interview in which the English writer Ann Quin is asked about a vision she'd had. How did she know it was God she had seen? "It's very difficult to talk about," she explains, "but I just know it couldn't be anything else. There was every possible landscape in the face: valleys, trees, mountains, hills."

Born in the seaside town of Brighton in 1936, Quin died in 1973 having walked into the water. According to one newspaper report, her body was found floating off the coast of nearby Shoreham "dressed only in panties." A fisherman had seen her strip down on a beach the night before. The article is brief—"Sea-death Woman Was Brighton Writer," it's called—but it includes a black-and-white photo of Quin almost smiling beneath a dark pixie cut. "She wrote many books," the article concludes, "including *Berg* and *Three*." In fact, at the time of her death, Quin had published four stylistically daring novels: *Berg, Three, Passages,* and *Tripticks*. She was only thirty-seven years old.

In a short piece called "Leaving School—XI," Quin's own version of her biography begins after her working-class mother packed her off to a convent school to rid her of a Sussex accent and transform her into "a lady." In the convent she felt trapped, sensed the devil always near, "hiding in the folds of black gowns," and developed "a death wish and a sense of sin. Also a great lust to find out, experience what evil really was." At the library, she read: Elizabethan drama, Chekhov, Hardy, Woolf. It was *The Waves* that showed her what writing could do. And how could it not? "The sun had not yet risen," Woolf begins. "The sea was indistinguishable from the sky, except that the sea was slightly creased as if a cloth had wrinkles in it. Gradually as the sky whitened a dark line lay on the horizon dividing the sea from the sky and the grey cloth became barred with thick strokes moving, one after another, beneath the surface, following each other, pursuing each other, perpetually."

Quin has been called "a bridge" between Woolf and Kathy Acker. Also: "Burrovian," "enigma-ridden," "understated," "tragic." At the time of her death, in addition to those four novels, she'd written a scattering of short stories not collected into a book.

In the introduction to her *New and Selected Stories,* Mexican writer Cristina Rivera Garza tells us that the term "short story" is simply "the name we have chosen to describe the production of the cultural and social space in which something hidden becomes visible, and therefore shared, but still as a secret." A story is therefore always two, one hidden inside the other.

Her own short stories often play with genre—fairy tales, detective stories, an anthropologist's field report—and she has also written poems, novels, memoir, criticism, an opera. In fact it's been said that Rivera Garza's writing explodes any notion of stability in genre, or in gender, or geopolitical borders, or narrative itself. Born on the southern bank of the Rio Grande, in Matamoros, Tamaulipas, in 1964, she earned a PhD in history in 1995 then published a work of fiction: *Nadie me verá llorar*. The historian and the writer of literature share two things, she has said, two important moments: first, when they enter the archive, excited but unknowing, and then when they discover the thing they did not know they were there to find, and they take it up, they choose it, to subvert it or betray it. "Writing is a community-making practice," she has said. "If we write, we write with others. Inescapably."

In her short story "The Date," Rivera Garza's detective asks for a room at a hotel called the Cosmos, a large room with a view. Right away he notices the smell. As he sifts through his notes on the case, a knock comes at the door, but the hallway is deserted. The carpet is thick and red. He is there to find a woman. He's been searching for seven months. This woman will be found, he thinks, in some vague "pre-human pose." He orders up veal, champagne. "Soft night noises." At last, he opens the closet. He pushes aside his clothes. Drills and removes a panel. He has opened a hole in the wall. It's a hole into another room and he pulls his body through.

The carpet is threadbare with flowers in Quin's "A Double Room." It's a seaside hotel with a pub nearby. Always, there is the sea, its crashing winter waves. "Waves of whiteness curled. Uncurled." We find the woman in the bathroom. Back inside the bedroom the man pours whisky into her tea. He pushes against her breasts. "Smell of sea. Fish. Tar." At last, it's time for sex. A lump. A knot. "His finger?" she thinks. It quickly feels like drowning. It can also feel like choking. She watches from up above, down there on the bed. You can leave your body any time. We walk the empty halls. The flowers in the hotel carpet are pink. Each door hides another sea; I mean, another room. We press our ears against two doors. "Sound of the sea," she says. "Sounds of other seas."

They make a plan to meet for the first time at a restaurant in a city in which neither of them lives or has ever lived, although, the first woman thinks, maybe that's wrong. Maybe the second woman once lived here.

The first woman is on the corner of a relatively quiet street, looking at a map on her phone, trying to understand which way she's meant to turn, when the second woman appears. The second woman is wearing a puffy orange jacket and asks for directions to the place they're meant to meet. "Well," the first woman says, "I am me and you are you." The second woman jumps up and claps her hands. "I didn't recognize you," she says. "You look so much older than in your pictures." The first woman doesn't know what to say to that. "Prettier!" the second woman says. "Older but prettier."

They order twenty-dollar bowls of soup. In terms of the décor, it's like someone stuffed a sixteenth-century French palace into a barn and then filled the barn with cacti. Velvet drapes help keep out the cold.

At some point the second woman says to the first, "I read your new book." But that is all she says about that. Later, she'll be, the second woman will, picked up in a limousine and taken to a party for a famous novelist who's very old; he's dying. "None of it seems real," the second woman says. Her own new book will be a miniseries soon.

Over coffee, the second woman says to the first, "If you write something with a real story and get it over two hundred pages, you can sell it. I promise. But if you keep writing little books that nobody reads, it's like 'what's the point,' you know? Like, truthfully, where's the impact?"

After lunch they walk to a store with bright white walls and a rubber tree plant. The second woman holds up a dress on a shiny metal hanger. "I wish you would let me buy you this dress," she says. "I would totally buy you this dress." But the second woman can't buy the dress because the first woman has killed her and left her body on the floor.

Back out on the street it smells like snow.

1.

One week it was alligators in frozen ponds. Their jaws rose out of the ice like those misty Chinese mountain peaks she'd once seen at an IMAX. The creatures looked both dead and in pain, but scientists called them "survival machines" and insisted they were asleep. The week before that it was a large disc of ice revolving at the confluence of two small rivers in Maine. It's not as if she went looking for them. But every week some new image got stuck at the front of her mind. That disc had looked exactly like the moon. The water was black and the moon of ice revolved for several days.

After work she reads a glossy magazine. She does not eat any dinner.

Across the street is an empty space where a building used to be, and on the floor beside her is another, smaller space.

2.

"In the novel I'm reading there's a character reading a book. Wait, let me back up. I couldn't sleep. I got up and checked the mousetraps, I had to pee, and then I got back in bed. I turned on the yellow lamp. A picture of a plant had held my page, a rubber tree plant, a Polaroid. So I'm reading in bed when outside my window a bird begins to sing, but it's pitch-black outside, it's midnight. Then I get to a sentence about how the narrator can't sleep. She turns on her bedside lamp and starts to read. So there we are, awake in bed and reading, this narrator and me, and something crazy happens; it's like I'm there, or like she's here, like something has fallen through. It's night and I'm reading a book, and inside my book it's night and a woman is reading a book. Then she starts reading out loud, fragments of lines that speak to her— 'violence, yes, but the acceptable face of violence, the kind of banal cruelty enacted within the family' and 'the hum of ordinary life' and 'the story of a woman who has lost something important but does not know exactly what'—and that's when I realize that I have read this book. Not the book I'm reading but the book inside my book, the one the narrator's reading from. That other book is also about a woman, one who tells her story through the story of another woman. So it's night and I'm holding a book, and inside my book it's night and there's a woman holding a book, and inside her book, which I have read, there's a woman writing a book about another woman's life. It's like all these two-dimensional images have suddenly been arranged inside a three-dimensional space. It all feels really intimate. But is the intimacy with the narrator or with the book in my hands? Or is it with the author of one or both of the books? Then it occurs to me that the intimacy is in those several quoted lines. That's what we all share. So I read the lines again, out loud myself this time, and then, satisfied, I move on to finish the scene. The narrator's boy comes into the room. He asks her what she's reading. She and the child talk, and that's when it's revealed that she is reading the other book in its original language, French, whereas all this time I've been reading everything in English. For some reason, this shocks me. Everything drains away. I feel stupid. I can't explain. I'm just sitting there on the bed."

3.

When she was little, alone in the house at night, she used to take a blade and cut away the bodies of the models in her mother's magazines. She'd leave the rooms and landscapes intact, but the people would be gone. After a while, it was as if she'd been cut away too, just a flat shape on the carpet where she and her material needs had been.

STORY WITH A HOLE

On page sixty-eight of a biography of the Shaker Mother Ann Lee, an elderly sister laments the fact that Shaker chairs now fetch a high price. They weren't built to be sold but sat in. She says, "I don't want to be remembered as a chair."

In the morning, I sit and stare. The day is already hot. I can feel my kid behind me—hair, juice, eyes. On the radio they say the fire is only 7 percent contained. A warbler on the feeder is whistling its brains out. Then my husband returns from wherever he's been and slams the garden gate.

At noon, like an omen, we find the back half of a black snake on the sidewalk.

Having finished the hole at last, I stand to one side and hose it. A Shaker brother once said: "It is the nature of all things to grow, and the faster they grow the worse they are." I lower in the pear tree. My kid flings fists of dirt.

Here's the thing about dinner—my husband isn't there.

Drinking alone on the porch swing, I read that Mother Lee believed in keeping the sexes apart. The sisters packaged seeds while the brethren tended the orchard, or the men built buckets while the women gathered nuts, then once each week they'd meet to dance, "swiftly passing and re-passing each other like clouds agitated in a mighty wind."

I take one pill—half purple, half pink.

Later, in his underwear, body clean, hair slick, my kid admits to swallowing a pit. It's a wicked kind of heat, and I turn on the fan in the corner. The blackout curtains smell of smoke. The moon is an orange-red. "What could happen?" he says. "I guess a plum tree will grow inside you," I say, flipping off the light. "I guess branches will grow out your ears and you'll blossom and smell very sweet and I'll plant you in the yard." Once, when I was ten or eleven, I put a cucumber in my vagina. I didn't do anything with it, just held it there, feeling strangely refreshed. "Don't be crazy, Mom," he whispers in the dark.

I finish the book in bed. It ends with a Shaker song: "To turn, turn will be our delight / Till by turning, turning we come round right."

The TV can switch itself off, thank god, still I wake in the dark to a man in blue shorts pulling a horse away from smoke. There's a prisoner fighting the fire in return for early release. His cheeks are streaked with ash. His mask reflects the flames. "Being a firefighter is a privilege," he says into the camera. "It makes you feel like you're part of a civilization." Then he turns into a line of burning trees.

POOL OF TEARS

(A PLAY IN ONE ACT)

> "What is it that story does not allow us to see?"
> —PARUL SEHGAL

Scene 1

> *The stage is a vast manmade lake surrounded on three sides by rolling hills and on the fourth by an unseen megadam. The surface of the lake is bright and blank, a mirror of the sky. There's a group of swimmers out on the lake, too far out to be clearly seen, and below them as they approach is the village or town or city that was swallowed when the megadam went in. Memories of this landscape have been lost. Who and what once lived there? Also lost when the dam was built: a forest. When the swimmers finally come into view, the audience members recognize them as characters from their dreams. Simultaneously, every member of the audience thinks of what Amitav Ghosh says about recognition*

near the start of The Great Derangement: "Recognition is famously a passage from ignorance
to knowledge," but one that "harks back to something prior," so that the knowledge we gain from
recognition "is not of the same kind as the dis-
covery of something new: it arises rather from
a renewed reckoning with a potentiality that lies
within oneself." Certain members of the audience
continue to think about Ghosh's book ("the challenges climate change poses for the contemporary
writer, although specific in some respects, are
also products of something broader and older
. . . they derive ultimately from the grid of literary forms and conventions that came to shape
the narrative imagination in precisely that period when the accumulation of carbon in the at-
mosphere was rewriting the destiny of the earth"),
while the rest watch and wait for whatever will
happen next.

Silence.

The group of swimmers has crossed the lake and
arrives CENTER STAGE. All the swimmers begin
to speak at once.

SWAN:

DUCK:

OWL:

MONKEY 1:

MONKEY 2:

GOOSE:

RAT:

DODO:

PIGEON:

SLOTH:

ALICE: Shortly after I first arrived at the Pool of Tears, I
           began to dream at night of a woman with the
           wings of a bird, or wrestling with a bird, its
           wings obscuring her face. Flying or falling
           through the air—I wasn't sure. I wasn't sure
           about much back then. One night I dreamed
           I had a wolf's head, but in the dream my head
           was only the drawing of the head of a wolf. It
           was my body, flesh and bone, with a scratchy
           pen-and-ink profile of the head of a wolf on my

shoulders. Inside this drawing of a wolf's head there was a circle, and inside that circle there was a second wolf, only that wolf was real and he was running fast.

(ALICE turns to GOOSE and listens.)
Tell them what was in the real wolf?

(ALICE turns back to the audience.)
There was a forest inside the wolf.

The swimmers have been treading water. It is difficult to give a speech while treading water and the swimmers are all slightly out of breath, except for DODO. *Now, still swimming, they exit* STAGE RIGHT.

(BLACKOUT)

Scene 2

The stage is empty and the water is unmoving. The surface of the lake is so blank, in fact, that the audience members feel invited to inscribe themselves upon it. In this way, the lake mirrors other landscapes, official and vernacular, that the audience members, in their lifetimes, have felt invited to inscribe themselves upon. One person sees himself as a glittering Jesus walking across its surface. Many picture jet skis or picnics on the shore. A few try to imagine the swallowed-up village or town or city; they wonder about the materials that might have been used for building the now-flooded homes (adobe or burnt clay or bamboo or concrete or wood or glass) and about the gardens (scrappy or lush, sustaining or aesthetic) and about the pathways (paved or unpaved, mapped or unmapped). Suddenly the swimmers are spotted, distant STAGE LEFT, *and the audience members recall the strange feeling of recognition they experienced the first time the swimmers came into view. As the swimmers approach this time, however, rather than Amitav Ghosh, everyone thinks about the Russian formalist critic Viktor Shklovsky and his different use of that same term: recognition. Arguing, in "Art as Device," that we too easily grow habituated to our lives, Shklovsky says: "in order to return sensation to our limbs, in order to make us feel objects, to make a stone feel stony, man has been given the tool of art. The purpose of art, then, is to lead us to a knowledge of a thing through the organ of sight instead of recognition." Sight as opposed to recognition. Certain audience members wonder if they shouldn't just leave. A few want to argue these possibly opposing positions, or whether or not they are opposing positions at all. The water begins to ripple as the swimmers draw near. A number of audience members suspect their earlier experience of recognition was completely beside the point. Perhaps this play has nothing to do with their dreams? Others decide that there is something they should be seeing that they have not yet seen.*

The group of swimmers has crossed the lake and arrives CENTER STAGE. *All the swimmers begin to speak at once.*

SWAN:

DUCK:

OWL:

MONKEY 1:

MONKEY 2:

GOOSE:

RAT:

DODO:

PIGEON:

SLOTH:

ALICE: The day I arrived at the Pool of Tears my cab driver was named David. On the radio in his cab, a man and a woman spoke of the New Avocado, recently engineered in order to have no pit. The pit, the radioman explained, was a waste of valuable time. The pit was an "unnecessary natural feature." And the greatest part, he said, was that now we could all stop cutting our hands trying to get it out. "Excuse me," I said, leaning forward from the backseat, "have you ever used a knife to remove the pit from an avocado?" David said he had. "Many times," he added. "And have you ever cut your hand taking out the pit?" Neither David nor I had ever cut our hand taking out a pit. David just shook his head. "Is there a . . . hole?" the woman asked. "No hole," said the radioman. "It's like it was never there at all." "No hole," the woman repeated. "No hole," she said again, and she sounded 100 percent relieved.

The swimmers have been treading water. It is difficult to give a speech while treading water and the swimmers are all slightly out of breath, ex-

cept for DODO. *Now, still swimming, they exit*
STAGE RIGHT.

(BLACKOUT)

Scene 3

The lights come up and the lake is motionless.
The audience shifts in their seats. Minutes pass.
Someone clears their throat. Minutes pass. Some-
one raises their hand. "Excuse me," that one
says, "but when a megadam goes in, what hap-
pens to the fertile soil of a river's forest flood-
plains?" The other members of the audience
shrug. No one is sure who is being asked or who
is supposed to answer. Then someone asks:
"What happens to the forest's roots, edible and
medicinal? The bees and all of their honey? Or
migratory birds?" Minutes pass. Another audi-
ence member asks: "What does an underwater
forest sound like? Do its branches creak in the
water's current as they once did in the wind?"
At that, everyone in the audience pictures the
forest beneath the lake; they picture it intact, still
growing, full of life, like any normal forest, ex-
cept all around the trees is water instead of air.
Someone asks: "Do orangutans sink or float?
How about butterflies? Big cats or wolves?" Then:

"Where did the people who lived here go? Where are their children, their farms?" An audience member says: "Does a dam increase, locally, the chance of earthquakes and landslides?" (The audience chants: It does.) "If rivers carry sediment, and if the sediment feeds the fish, and if the sediment feeds the vegetation along the river's banks, then when you stop the sediment, do you stop the river? Is the river dead?" (The audience chants: It is.) "Can a megadam snuff out an entire endangered species?" (The audience chants: It can.) "If you clear or drown the forest, doesn't that in turn affect the climate, leading to more and prolonged droughts, and won't that affect how much water there is to power the dams you built?" (The audience chants: It will.) "What of the forest spirits, the forest gods?" (All gone. Destroyed.) The audience is on its feet. A march to the dam is planned. Certain members have markers and cardboard, and they commence the making of signs. Just then, STAGE LEFT, *the swimmers come into view. "Look!" someone cries. Too far off to be clearly distinguished, yet the sight of the swimmers on the lake causes the audience to fall silent. Minutes pass. People begin returning to their seats. The water ripples. Someone coughs. Someone blows their nose.*

The group of swimmers has crossed the lake and arrives CENTER STAGE. *All the swimmers begin to speak at once.*

SWAN:

DUCK:

OWL:

MONKEY 1:

MONKEY 2:

GOOSE:

RAT:

DODO:

PIGEON:

SLOTH:

ALICE: Later, I realized I'd seen something like that wolf's head with a wolf inside a circle inside it and a forest inside the wolf in, of all places, an illustration attached to an essay about

Mikhail Bakhtin's theories of the novel: "the only genre born of this new world and in total affinity with it." Of course he wrote that way back in 1941 and meant the new world then, the one around him, post Industrial Revolution, post atomic theory, and not the new world now, around me, with all its newer newness, among which the New Avocado. I suppose this means we'd need a newer new genre now? One of Bakhtin's contemporaries said that a book is a machine for thinking. So what kind of machine do *we* need? Anyway, like I said, I didn't remember where I'd first seen that drawing of a wolf until much later, and even then I wasn't sure how or why the image made its way through the twisted corridors of my brain, disentangling itself from an essay by someone whose name I can't recall, an essay I only know had something to do with the literary critic Mikhail Bakhtin and his ideas about the novel ("time, as it were, thickens, takes on flesh . . . likewise, space becomes charged and responsive to the movements of time"), getting attached instead to a dream dreamt in my first days at the Pool of Tears.

The swimmers have been treading water. It is difficult to give a speech while treading water and the swimmers are all slightly out of breath, except for DODO. *Now, still swimming, they exit* STAGE RIGHT.

(BLACKOUT)

Scene 4

A motionless surface, a mirror. The swimmers appear, STAGE LEFT, *but too far out to be clearly seen. Perhaps, the audience thinks, we shouldn't be so focused on vision, on sight. Perhaps instead we should listen. So the audience members listen. But everything is silent. They cannot hear a thing. "Say something!" someone cries. "What do you want from us?" someone shouts. The lake does not reply. Then one audience member stands and approaches the shoreline. They are holding a thick black-and-white book called* What Is Poetry? (Just Kidding, I Know You Know). *Having reached the shore, they turn and begin to read from an interview in which the American novelist and critic Samuel R. Delany interviews himself. "It's called 'A Silent Interview with Samuel R. Delany,'" the audience member explains. "Not because Delany refuses to answer his own questions, but because one need not make a sound to answer and question*

*oneself." The audience member begins to read:
"Since Wagner at least, silence has been consid-
ered the proper mode in which to appreciate the
work of art: Wagner was the first major artist
to forbid talking in the theater during his—" "I
don't understand!" someone interrupts as the
water begins to ripple. "Are you saying that this
lake is a work of art?"*

*The group of swimmers has crossed the lake and
arrives* CENTER STAGE. *All the swimmers begin
to speak at once.*

SWAN:

DUCK:

OWL:

MONKEY 1:

MONKEY 2:

GOOSE:

RAT:

DODO:

PIGEON:

SLOTH:

ALICE: Even as I dreamed of the wolf with a forest inside a wolf inside its head, there were also all those dreams about the woman and the bird: a woman with the wings of a bird or a bird obscuring her face. Over many nights, that image began to change. One night I saw a woman's bodiless head with a bird perched on her chin. In that iteration, it seemed the bird had won. Another night it was all woman but with the feet of a bird. Eventually, bird and woman settled into a routine: they swam the lake at night. I swim during the day, of course, and in this way it was as if I were always swimming, day and night, back and forth atop the forest, the town. Still, I never saw her face. Then, one night, I dreamed I was seated in the audience, here.

(ALICE points into the audience.)

The woman and the bird swam up to the stage. Treading water, she turned to me. I recognized her immediately. "The huia," she said, "was a bird endemic to New Zealand." "Hold up," I said, "is this a huia?" pointing to the bird. But the woman carried on. "One of the most fascinating things about the huia was the sexual dimorphism of its beak: the male's was short and straight, whereas the female's was long and down-arching. Crow-sized, the huia had dark metallic feathers with ivory tips and orange wattles. But after centuries of accumulated human arrival, the huia went extinct." She stopped talking but continued treading water. I thought it must be the end of her performance, so I began to clap. Then she went on: "In the 1990s, the British composer David Hindley made a new kind of music using a recording of an elderly Māori man named Hēnare Hāmana whistling the huia's song. Hāmana had heard and learned the huia's call as a boy, and he'd whistled it for the news in 1954. Hindley took that old recording, plus written descriptions of the huia's song comparing it to the calls of New Zealand's other birds, plus recordings of certain birds still living on the islands and, inside his computer, he recreated, or 'recreated,' the largely forgotten singing of a mostly forgotten bird." She stopped talking. I thought it must be the end of her performance, so I began to clap. Then she went on: "Hindley's rendition lasts five minutes. In it you hear the huia's song against the sonic backdrop of the forest in which it once lived." Suddenly the theater was filled with the sound of bird-song, bird after bird, the sounds of many birds in many trees: a forest. I had no way of knowing if this was the music that Hindley had manufactured or a field recording of some other place and its song or even the sound of the forest inside the head of the wolf. "Hey, are these birds extinct?" I said. But the bird and the woman were swimming away.

The swimmers have been treading water. It is difficult to give a speech while treading water and the swimmers are all slightly out of breath, except for DODO. *Now, still swimming, they exit* STAGE RIGHT.

(BLACKOUT)

Scene 5

"I don't know about you," someone finally says, "but I haven't understood a word they've said." "Me neither!" someone shouts. "I don't even think they're talking." "It's boring!" someone says. "Except for the one called Alice." "Only the girl!" "The one with the bow in her hair!" "That big bird with the ugly face never even opens its beak." "Dodo!" someone shouts. Then the swim-

mers appear, STAGE LEFT. *They are farther away than ever. The audience, exhausted, settles down to wait. Minutes pass. The sky is unchanged.* "Do you hear that?" *someone finally asks.* "Is it a train?" *says someone else.* "It sounds like it's coming from under the lake," *adds another. The water starts to ripple, though the swimmers are still far out.* "That's not a train," *somebody says. The ground has started to shake. The lake is like a bowl of water being carried by a child. Then a wave crests* CENTER STAGE *and splashes onto the floor.* "Is this still part of the play?" *someone asks.* "Wait, is this actual water?" "Earthquake!" *someone cries. The theater is filling up. The noise is monumental. As audience members rush for the doors several people get trampled to death and several people drown. The water churns with branches and mud and smashes against the walls. It's dark inside the theater. The lights have shorted out. Someone is screaming,* "Help me! Help!" *Most of them do escape. They run out to the parking garage and get in their cars and go. Eventually everything quiets. For several days after, the theater is filled with the lake. Then, inch by inch, the water begins to retreat, until the only thing left in the theater is mud and corpses and trash: candy wrappers, water bottles, a stack of soggy signs. The sky is blank, the lake a mirror.*

Hours pass.

The group of swimmers has crossed the lake and arrives CENTER STAGE. *All the swimmers begin to speak at once.*

SWAN:

DUCK:

OWL:

MONKEY 1:

MONKEY 2:

GOOSE:

RAT:

DODO:

PIGEON:

SLOTH:

ALICE: I wasn't sure what to make of the story the woman told me, but it got me thinking about a book I'd read before I came to the Pool of Tears. In *Slow Violence and the Environmentalism of the Poor,* Rob Nixon addresses the ways in which contemporary writing might engage environmental catastrophe and injustice. He argues that in this regard nonfiction has a "special allure" due to its "robust adaptability, imaginative and political, as well as to its information-carrying capacity and its aura of the real." Of course I hadn't known, as the woman was speaking, whether or not her story was fictional or fact-based. So for several nights before going to sleep I read up on the huia. In the course of my nightly research I came across a quote by the wildlife ecologist and poet Julianne Warren, who describes the recording of Hēnare Hāmana's whistling as "an extinct birdman remembered song saved in a machine for passing on." It was the "bird-man" that caught my attention, its implication that the song Hāmana whistled wasn't exactly a bird's and was not exactly a man's.

"Fish have been my teachers," writes the Métis anthropologist and scholar Zoe Todd in "Fish, Kin and Hope: Tending to Water Violations in Amiskwaciwâskahikan and Treaty Six Territory." She goes on to say that her grandfather "was animated by a different animal, horses." Living in rental houses on the prairie, he "drew dream horses right onto the walls." Even after his death, Todd writes, "those horses keep running wild in those houses." He made houses with prairies inside them. We make machines for remembering what we loved.

NOTES & ACKNOWLEDGMENTS

Many references and sources are named directly in my writing, but I'd like to name a few below that might otherwise go unnoticed, and to express my appreciation for the editors who previously published certain of these pieces:

NOCTURNE
Several lines are quoted from Katherine Mansfield's "Prelude," which is where Kezia and the headless duck are from. In writing this, I returned again and again to Whistler's 1875 painting *Nocturne in Black and Gold—The Falling Rocket.*

First appeared in *Conjunctions,* with thanks to Bradford Morrow.

THESE BAD THINGS
Dedicated to my former student, the late Zishan (Simoner) Zhao, who was a promising young writer. This piece quotes a line about stars from Francis William Bourdillon's "The Night Has a Thousand Eyes."

First appeared online at *Guernica,* with thanks to Meakin Armstrong.

INSTALLATION

This piece is in conversation with Virginia Woolf's "In the Orchard" and Anna Kavan's "A Bright Green Field," in addition to Yayoi Kusama's dots.

LOST LUNAR APOGEE

The poem with snow falling inside a bookcase is based on Wang Jiaxin's "Tangerine," translated by Diana Shi and George O'Connell. The line quoted in the final paragraph is from Alasdair Gray's "The Star."

First appeared in *The White Review,* with thanks to Francesca Wade.

MY WONDERFUL DESCRIPTION OF FLOWERS

The story the narrator listens to is Carmen Maria Machado's "Blur"; the story she remembers near the end is based on Haruki Murakami's "Sleep," translated by Jay Rubin. The book about the painter is *Being Here Is Everything: The Life of Paula Modersohn-Becker* by Marie Darrieussecq, translated by Penny Hueston. *Daphne* is based on the indie video game *Dear Esther.*

First published in *The New Yorker,* with thanks to Cressida Leyshon.

SIXTY-SIX DRESSES I HAVE READ

First appeared online at *Fence,* with thanks to Jason Zuzga.

A PICTURE HELD US CAPTIVE

First published, in a slightly different iteration, as a full-color, illustrated chapbook from Image Text Ithaca press, with thanks to Catherine Taylor, Elana Schlenker, and Nicholas Muellner.

ONE WOMAN AND TWO GREAT MEN

First appeared in the *Chicago Review,* with thanks to Max McKenna.

ACORN

First published online at *The New Yorker,* with thanks to Cressida Leyshon.

NOT WRITING

The Duras line was translated by Mark Polizzotti. The Lispector line was translated by Giovanni Pontiero. The lines about soup and anguish are in response to lines about soup and anguish in Amina Cain's *A Horse at Night.* The conversation quoted from first appeared online at *BOMB*: "Danielle Dutton and Richard Kraft: Magpies, Comics, Paradoxes, and the Spirit of Disruption." Two quoted lines are from Renee Gladman's 2021 Bagley Wright lectures, collectively titled "Am I a Fiction?" The book about the witch is *Lolly Willowes* by Sylvia Townsend Warner.

SOMEHOW

The Buddhist teacher who told the anecdote about Laurie Anderson is Jack Kornfield. The painter from the Eileen Myles essay is George Kuchar, and the essay is "Brothers 'N' Sons & Female Heroes: Mike & George."

First appeared in *The Paris Review,* with thanks to Nicole Rudick.

A DOUBLE ROOM

Some material in this piece first appeared in my introduction to the 2022 reissue of Ann Quin's novel *Tripticks* by And Other Stories, with thanks to Jennifer Hodgson and Jeremy M. Davies.

TO WANT FOR NOTHING

The book the character is reading in the second part is based on Valeria Luiselli's *Lost Children Archive;* the book inside it is Nathalie Léger's *Supplément à la vie de Barbara Loden.*

An earlier iteration appeared as catalogue text for Laura Letinsky's exhibition of photographs, *To Want for Nothing,* at DOCUMENT gallery in Chicago in the spring of 2019.

STORY WITH A HOLE

First appeared in an earlier iteration and under a different title in *Faultline,* with thanks to Michelle Latiolais and Kathleen Mackay.

POOL OF TEARS

This piece is named for and takes inspiration from Kiki Smith's *Pool of Tears 2 (after Lewis Carroll)*. The Shklovsky was translated by Benjamin Sher.

First published in *Conjunctions*, with thanks to Bradford Morrow.

*

Thank you to all those named above (and to every artist and writer named elsewhere in this collection). Thanks also to my agents Cynthia Cannell and Harriet Moore, as well as David Evans, Charlotte Kelly, and Caroline Sincerbeaux. Thanks to Ally Findley and Anna Morrison. Endless love to my family and friends (you know who you are). Thank you, finally, to the entire staff at Coffee House Press, for all the work you do, for keeping to the mission.

*

The prairie is one of the least conserved habitats on the planet. Missouri, where I live, was once covered in many millions of acres of prairie. No more than fifty thousand scattered acres, called "remnant prairies," remain. Half of my proceeds from the sale of this book will go to the Missouri Prairie Foundation, which works to conserve remaining prairies and native grasslands.

Coffee House Press began as a small letterpress operation in 1972 and has grown into an internationally renowned nonprofit publisher of literary fiction, essay, poetry, and other work that doesn't fit neatly into genre categories.

Coffee House is both a publisher and an arts organization. Through our *Books in Action* program and publications, we've become interdisciplinary collaborators and incubators for new work and audience experiences. Our vision for the future is one where a publisher is a catalyst and connector.

LITERATURE
is not the same thing as
PUBLISHING

FUNDER ACKNOWLEDGMENTS

Coffee House Press is an internationally renowned independent book publisher and arts nonprofit based in Minneapolis, MN; through its literary publications and *Books in Action* program, Coffee House acts as a catalyst and connector—between authors and readers, ideas and resources, creativity and community, inspiration and action.

Coffee House Press books are made possible through the generous support of grants and donations from corporations, state and federal grant programs, family foundations, and the many individuals who believe in the transformational power of literature. This activity is made possible by the voters of Minnesota through a Minnesota State Arts Board Operating Support grant, thanks to the legislative appropriation from the Arts and Cultural Heritage Fund. Coffee House also receives major operating support from the Amazon Literary Partnership, Jerome Foundation, Literary Arts Emergency Fund, McKnight Foundation, and the National Endowment for the Arts (NEA). To find out more about how NEA grants impact individuals and communities, visit www.arts.gov.

Coffee House Press receives additional support from Bookmobile; the Buckley Charitable Fund; Dorsey & Whitney LLP; the Gaea Foundation; the Schwab Charitable Fund; and the U.S. Bank Foundation.

THE PUBLISHER'S CIRCLE OF COFFEE HOUSE PRESS

Publisher's Circle members make significant contributions to Coffee House Press's annual giving campaign. Understanding that a strong financial base is necessary for the press to meet the challenges and opportunities that arise each year, this group plays a crucial part in the success of Coffee House's mission.

Recent Publisher's Circle members include many anonymous donors, Kathy Arnold, Patricia A. Beithon, Andrew Brantingham & Rita Farmer, Kelli & Dave Cloutier, Theodore Cornwell, Jane Dalrymple-Hollo, Mary Ebert & Paul Stembler, Jennifer Egan, Kamilah Foreman, Eva Galiber, Jocelyn Hale & Glenn Miller Charitable Fund of the Minneapolis Foundation, Roger Hale & Nor Hall, William Hardacker, Randy Hartten & Ron Lotz, Carl & Heidi Horsch, Amy L. Hubbard & Geoffrey J. Kehoe Fund of the St. Paul & Minnesota Foundation, Hyde Family Charitable Fund, Kenneth & Susan Kahn, the Kenneth Koch Literary Estate, Cinda Kornblum, the Lenfestey Family Foundation, Sarah Lutman & Rob Rudolph, Carol & Aaron Mack, Gillian McCain, Mary & Malcolm McDermid, Daniel N. Smith III & Maureen Millea Smith, Vance Opperman, Mr. Pancks' Fund in memory of Graham Kimpton, Alan Polsky, Robin Preble, Ronald Restrepo & Candace S. Baggett, Steve Smith, Lynne Stanley, Jeffrey Sugerman & Sarah Schultz, Paul Thissen, Grant Wood, and Margaret Wurtele.

For more information about the Publisher's Circle and other ways to support Coffee House Press books, authors, and activities, please visit www.coffeehousepress.org/pages/donate or contact us at info@coffeehousepress.org.

COLOPHON

Prairie, Dresses, Art, Other was designed by Danielle Dutton. Text is set in Minion Pro.